"A date? Someone you're serious about?" Stuart asked.

Elaine started adding one and one together and came up with a cupid in the woodpile. "A patient invited me for dinner."

"That patient wouldn't happen to be my sister, would it?" Stuart asked. Before she could answer, he added, "The same sister whose voice was quivering with excitement when she invited her brother to dinner?"

Elaine nodded. "Sorry. Sometimes my patients think a midwife should have a husband and a flock of kids waiting at home. When I don't live up to their expectations, they get this uncontrollable urge to rectify the situation. I'll call your sister and make some excuse."

"And spoil her evening? She's probably at home keeping one eye on the oven while she oils up the shotgun...."

Dear Reader,

Each and every month, to satisfy your taste for substantial, memorable, emotion-packed stories of life and love, of dreams and possibilities, Silhouette brings you six extremely *Special Editions*.

This month, to mark our continually renewed commitment to bring you the very best and the brightest in contemporary romance writing, Silhouette *Special Edition* features a distinguished lineup of authors you've chosen as your favorites. Nora Roberts, Linda Howard, Tracy Sinclair, Curtiss Ann Matlock, Jo Ann Algermissen and Emilie Richards each deliver a powerful new romantic novel, along with a personal message to you, the reader.

Keep a sharp eye out for all six—you won't want to miss this dazzling constellation of romance stars. And stay with us in the months to come, because each and every month, Silhouette *Special Edition* is dedicated to becoming more special than ever.

From all the authors and editors of *Special Edition*, Warmest wishes,

Leslie Kazanjian
Senior Editor

JO ANN ALGERMISSEN
Blue Emeralds

Silhouette Special Edition

Published by Silhouette Books New York

America's Publisher of Contemporary Romance

SILHOUETTE BOOKS
300 East 42nd St., New York, N.Y. 10017

ISBN: 0-373-09455-8

First Silhouette Books printing May 1988

Books by Jo Ann Algermissen

Silhouette Desire

Naughty, but Nice #246
Challenge the Fates #276
Serendipity Samantha #300
Hank's Woman #318
Made in America #361
Lucky Lady #409

Silhouette Special Edition

Purple Diamonds #374
Blue Emeralds #455

JO ANN ALGERMISSEN

believes in love, be it romantic love, sibling love, parental love or love of books. She's given and received them all. Ms. Algermissen and her husband of more than twenty years live on Kiawah Island in South Carolina with their two children, a weimaraener and three horses. In such beautiful surroundings with such a loving family, she considers herself one lucky lady. Jo Ann Algermissen also writes under the pseudonym Anna Hudson.

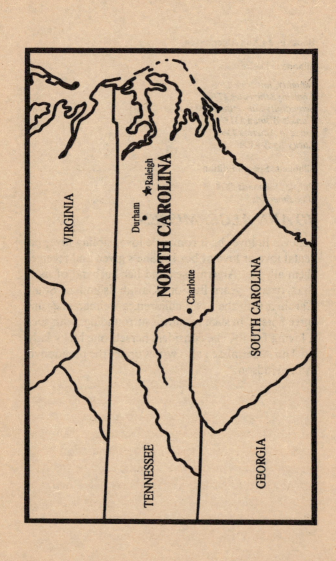

Chapter One

It's a girl!" Elaine Kramer declared, placing the newborn baby in her mother's arms. "Exactly what you wanted."

Thrilled, Trey Glenn, the new father, smiled at his wife and his tiny child. "You were magnificent. She's magnificent!" His voice was high-pitched with excitement. "I never thought I'd be able to do it."

"All three of you were magnificent," Elaine agreed. Trey had helped immensely with the delivery. Although Tammy had been mentally and physically prepared for the delivery, there had been a moment when panic had threatened to override the training she'd received. Solid as a rock, Trey had coached Tammy by taking deep breaths, slowly exhaling, then panting rapidly, until his wife had been in control again. He'd been part of it all; from conception to delivery.

Pride glowed in Elaine's blue-green eyes as she watched Trey kiss Tammy's forehead, then their child's tiny cheek.

Often Elaine was asked, "Why'd you become a midwife?" If the people asking could observe the expressions on the parents' faces after they'd worked together to bring new life into the world, they'd have their answer.

Magnificent was too ordinary a word for the experience.

Miraculous was more like it, Elaine mused, grinning as she watched the father, mother and child. Truly a miracle.

As though Tammy had heard Elaine's thoughts, she said to Trey, her voice trembling, "It is a miracle. I'd have fallen apart if you hadn't been here to help me." Her eyelids drooped. Fatigued but euphoric, she touched the fine dark hair on the baby's head. "She's perfect, isn't she?"

"Just like her mom," Trey answered. "Beautiful. You were never more beautiful to me than you are right now."

Love flowed between husband and wife, spilling over onto Elaine, warming her. She watched as both parents counted the baby's fingers and toes.

"Everything where it's supposed to be?" Elaine teased pulling the sheet back in place after a final check on the new mother.

"Ten of each. Lord, her hands are so tiny." Trey's smile widened as the tiny fingers curled around his thumb.

Somehow Elaine felt certain that within twenty-four hours the child would reverse that situation. She'd have her father wrapped around her little finger in no time.

Unobtrusively, she checked Tammy's vital signs. Pulse normal. Color good. She completed her mental checklist. Both mother and child were progressing normally. Later she'd document the delivery on Tammy's chart.

"Tired?" Elaine asked.

Tammy nodded. "But happy."

Elaine knew that what her patient needed at the moment was sleep. The need for food, fluids and quiet, in that order, would follow later. She signaled Trey with her eyes, glancing from the baby toward the door.

Trey nodded, but hesitated before picking up his child.

"You know how," Elaine chided him with a smile. "I promise she won't break. She's as resilient as the baby doll you practiced with at the clinic."

Tammy's sleepy smile of encouragement was all it took for Trey to regain his confidence in his ability to take care of the baby. "Mind if I show off the baby to your mother?" he asked.

Yawning, Tammy shook her head. "I think I'll take a little catnap, if it's okay."

Elaine pulled the sheet and the thin blanket up to Tammy's shoulders. "I'll check back with you later. Don't worry about anything. Rest."

Nature's prescription for recovery required rest. From experience with other young mothers, Elaine knew her patient would doze on and off throughout the remainder of the day. The first two or three days Tammy would be reflective, dependent on Trey and her mother. As she rested and nursed her baby, she'd ponder her new role, comparing it with her pregnancy and the birth experience.

Within the week she'd begin to take hold, initiating action, impatient with her physical discomfort. Because she knew Tammy, Elaine wasn't worried about the infant's needs being met. From the moment Tammy had walked into the Mother's Clinic, she'd been determined to learn all she could about prenatal care.

The third week after delivery was when Elaine would make frequent checks on Tammy. Often a new mother seemed almost to grieve over the absence of the infant within her womb. Tears, irritability, confusion and an inability to make decisions were the clues to watch for.

Elaine's mind was weeks ahead of her footsteps as she followed Trey from the bedroom into the living room.

"My new grandchild?" Mrs. Bennett asked, extending her arms toward the small bundle. Trey grudgingly relinquished his daughter. "Oh, isn't she a sweetheart?"

"One of the prettiest babies I've delivered," Elaine agreed wholeheartedly. Noting the flash of concern on Tammy's mother's face, she added, "Tammy is resting. She's an excellent patient. I'm very proud of her."

"I've waited a long time for this little darlin'," Mrs. Bennett crooned, drawing the child to her bosom.

"You're going to look like a little princess in the christening gown I embroidered for you." She glanced up at Elaine. "Tammy said they've asked you to be her godmother. My daughter has grown very close to you over the past few months."

"The feeling is mutual," Elaine assured the woman. "I feel as though we're friends rather than midwife and patient."

That often happened, much to Elaine's delight. Two years ago, when she'd first moved to the small town near Gaston Lake in North Carolina, she'd chosen the area because of its distance from Nashville, Tennessee, and because of its isolation. No one had known her. No one had stared at her pityingly. No one had spoken soft, sympathetic words about her rapidly deteriorating marriage. No one had felt awkward because they knew she had failed to conceive while her patients had blossomed during their pregnancies.

Anonymity had given her breathing space, time to get her life back in order.

The day she'd nailed the handcarved Mother's Clinic sign outside the building she'd refurbished, she'd known she'd grown beyond that stressful period of her life.

Granted, unlike most of the town's residents, she couldn't trace her roots back through the years of North Carolina history. Her parents and grandparents and great-grandparents hadn't provided her with aunts, uncles and cousins who lived nearby. She'd made her own family: she was godmother to seven thriving children.

She likened herself to an adopted child—special because she'd been chosen to be part of a family. Now she was part of the community, and they were a vital part of her.

Elaine glanced at her watch and stretched, then rubbed the back of her neck.

Trey saw her and said, "It's been a long night. You aren't going to the clinic this morning, are you?"

Nodding, Elaine moved her head from side to side to relieve the kinks. "Thanks for your concern, but don't worry about me." A slow smile curved her pale lips. "For some reason, most of my patients choose midnight to begin labor. I wasn't at the clinic yesterday, so I have to be there today."

"How about a cup of coffee and some homemade cinnamon rolls before you leave?" Mrs. Bennett offered graciously.

"Thanks, but one more cup of coffee and you'll hear me sloshing as I walk." Her eyes followed Trey's heavy footsteps as he returned to the bedroom. He was so wiped out that his manners had slipped, which was highly unusual. Trey never let her leave without walking her to her car. "Your granddaughter will sleep most of the day. Call if you need me."

She bade Mrs. Bennett goodbye and started for the front door, then realized she'd almost left her medical bag.

But Trey hadn't forgotten. While she'd been talking to his mother-in-law, he'd retrieved her black satchel from the bedroom. "She's sound asleep. You must be sleepwalking to forget your bag. Try to catch a couple of winks sometime during the day, would you? I'd hate to have to call a doctor for the midwife." He opened the front door, gesturing with a swing of her medical bag for her to precede him.

She noticed the dark smudges beneath his eyes. He needed to follow his own advice. "Don't bother escorting me to the car."

"That's the least I can do after all you've done for us."

Arguing was pointless. Trey abided by the code of Southern chivalry. It would take her longer to convince him that he needed rest as badly as she did than it would for him to accompany her to the car.

As they walked across the porch, down the steps and along the sidewalk, which was edged with colorful summer flowers, Elaine gave Trey a few last-minute instructions, finishing with, "Day or night, don't hesitate to call me." She patted the beeper on the belt of her polished-cotton slacks. "I'm never farther away than the nearest telephone."

Trey tried unsuccessfully to stifle a yawn. He gave her a sheepish smile when he saw her attempt to hide her own yawn. Opening the door of her Bronco and placing the medical bag in the back seat, he asked, "Midwife's motto?"

Elaine shrugged. "My motto. The two of you are new at being parents. I've been around long enough to see just about every crisis that can occur." Always the midwife, never the mother, she thought unexpectedly. Good Lord, she must be running short on adrenaline to have let that thought cross her mind.

She closed the door and started the engine. "See you tomorrow," she said to Trey. In the rearview mirror she saw him wave, grin and sprint up the path. She envied him his stamina. Elaine had been looking forward to the solitary drive back into town, hoping it would give her a chance to wind down. Rolling hills, pastures dotted with cattle, fields with chest-high corn, nature at its summer best—the scenery should have soothed her. Instead, she felt unaccountably restless, keyed up, when she should have been fighting not to fall asleep at the wheel.

She'd pushed both her mind and body too hard in the last forty-eight hours.

Memories that she'd relegated to the farthest recesses of her mind crowded forward relentlessly. Mental images of Joe, her ex-husband, flashed on the windshield. A voice from the past shouted recriminations louder than easy-listening music playing on the radio.

Elaine yanked the steering wheel to the right and pulled off the road. She raked her fingers lethargically through her short dark hair. Nagging stress-related aches and pains caused her brow to wrinkle.

Months had come and gone since she'd thought about Joe or Nashville or the failure of her marriage and her inability to have a child. Why now? she wondered. Delayed reaction? Ridiculous, she answered silently. Maybe it was seeing how ecstatic the Glenns were with their new baby that had her dredging up unfulfilled dreams.

Sighing, she slumped deeper into the seat. She knew better than to try to repress her thoughts. If she bottled up her feelings, the only result would be nightmares that left her pillow damp and her heart thudding like a wild thing. The clinic would have to wait while she sifted through those emotions in the bright light of day.

"Okay," she muttered, consciously removing the mental roadblocks she used to keep herself in control. "There's nothing back there that can hurt me now."

She lowered her hands to the vinyl seat. There had been a time when her fingers would have trembled or automatically balled into fists. Insight into her fears had taken her beyond those instinctive reactions. Her hands rested on the seat, limp. Memories, like childhood bogeymen, couldn't hurt her unless she let them.

Calmly she listened as Joe's past grievances echoed within her mind.

"We planned on having a family."

Those were the first words she'd heard when she'd awakened from the anesthetic the surgeon had given her. Joe's monotone recrimination had revealed a wealth of barely suppressed feelings: hurt, anger, disbelief. After all, he was a healthy man in the prime of life. Making babies certainly wasn't his problem. Why wasn't she being her usual cooperative self? She'd never denied him anything. Why was her body conspiring against him?

Weak, willing to assume guilt for her irregular monthly cycle, the tubular pregnancy and the resulting surgery, in desperation she'd offered him the only thing she could: hope.

"I can still get pregnant," she'd replied, teary-eyed. "We just have to try harder."

And they had tried. She'd quit her nursing job at the hospital and isolated herself from her friends and family. For a whole year, charts and thermometers were her closest companions. When the mercury rose a fraction of a degree, she'd call Joe. With the precision of a well-planned real estate deal, he'd arrive, take care of business and depart.

Once, when she'd set aside her guilt and worked up enough nerve to complain about his clinical approach to lovemaking, he'd stared at her as though she'd sprouted two heads, each with inch-long fangs protruding beneath fire-breathing nostrils.

He refused even to dignify her complaint with an answer. Nor did he change. She was a nurse. She of all people should know that making babies didn't require cuddling and stroking. Softly spoken words of love hadn't helped in the past, so why bother now? Her husband was there for one reason and one reason only—to impregnate his wife.

His desire for a child became an obsession that didn't allow room for frivolous intimacy.

Frustrated by month after month of being at her beck and call without results, he'd finally shouted, "I want a child. I'm going to get one. With or without you."

Elaine's sole comfort was knowing that Joe's sense of honor would keep him from carrying out his thinly veiled threat. Selfish? Perhaps, but she clung tenaciously to the hope of getting pregnant as though it were a lifeline to her sanity.

Inevitably, as each month passed, the threads of hope and love and honor that held their marriage together frayed, then unraveled. By then her self-esteem had been thoroughly shredded by Joe's accusing glares and silences. The price for loving him had become too great. She was barely able to scrape up enough courage and pride to divorce him with dignity.

Ironically, when the process-server discreetly served him the papers at his real estate office, he rushed home as though she'd called him to make love, as she had so many times during the past year. The moment she heard him enter the house in the middle of the day, she knew he'd received the papers from her attorney.

She watched in grim silence as he went into their bedroom and hurriedly packed his bags. Hurting too much to cry, she wondered how a person could bleed to death internally and remain standing rigid. Rigor mortis before death? Near hysteria, she choked back a burst of anguished laughter.

When he'd finished packing, Joe crossed to the front door, luggage in hand, and stopped. Setting his bags down, he turned toward her. "I loved you," he said, regret constricting his throat and strangling his words. His eyes filled with moisture. He cleared his throat and continued. "I want you to know I hate myself for what I've put you through. You have every right to call me every rotten name in the book." He took a deep breath, as though he were waiting for her to start a vicious tirade. When she remained silent, his voice dropped to a whisper. "In a very special way, I'll always love you." He paused, then slammed the flat of his hand against his thigh and asked rhetorically, "Why is life so *damned* unfair?"

Unable to bear his pain or answer his question, Elaine turned toward the wall and pressed her fist to her mouth, squeezing her eyes shut until black specks danced in front of them. Hot tears trickled down her throat like acid rain. Over the sound of the blood pounding in her ears, she heard his footsteps approaching her. She shook her head violently, clamping her teeth on her lower lip to stop herself from begging him to stay—to give her one more chance to bear him a child. Keeping her face averted, she raised her arm and stuck out her hand to stop him from touching her. She'd shatter into nothingness if he touched her.

He didn't.

"I won't fight the divorce. Goodbye, Elaine."

Sighing deeply, knowing the worst of the memories were over, Elaine wiped a thin sheen of perspiration from her forehead. The summer sun bathed her face as the temperature in the parked vehicle soared to the ninety-degree mark. She could have pulled the car back onto the lane and blocked the final memory of her marriage, but she didn't. This one last time, she would allow the past to affect her present life.

She recalled the day the final divorce papers had arrived. She'd held them in her hand and sobbed—for him, for herself, for all the dreams they'd shared and lost.

Those were the last tears she'd shed. Slowly she'd mended her broken heart. Time was a great healer. Changing locations had helped, too. The Smoky Mountains, a towering granite wall, physically separated her home state from where she'd taken up residence. She'd made a new life for herself here in North Carolina, a life centered around the Mother's Clinic.

She didn't delude herself about why she'd become a midwife. Yes, she realized that she got a vicarious thrill each time a healthy baby was born. Vanquished hopes of having a child of her own were replaced by joy when she helped other women to have their babies. If anything, her inability to have a child made her more sensitive toward expectant mothers and fathers.

Elaine straightened behind the steering wheel. She was comfortable with her present circumstances. She'd survived. One bad experience had shaken her self-esteem, but it hadn't destroyed it. Of course, she mused, there were times when she felt lonely. Normal people needed companionship—be they male or female.

She mulled over that thought, liking the idea of being a "normal woman."

During the past few months she'd recovered to the point of accepting a few dates. Whether by design or destiny, her dates had remained casual acquaintances. The situation hadn't arisen where she'd have felt honor-bound to reveal the fact that she'd been married and divorced, much less the reasons behind the divorce.

Should that situation change, she knew exactly how she'd handle it. Before she became too involved, she'd simply state the facts. If the man couldn't deal with her inability to have children, then that was his problem. She'd freed herself from the dismal past by having enough gumption to call it quits; she sure as hell wasn't going to shackle herself to a bleak future by avoiding the issue.

With that thought firmly in mind, she flicked the ignition key. Over the roar of the Bronco's engine, she heard her beeper sound. Elaine pushed the button and read the phone number on the gadget's digital display.

Uh-oh, she thought, pulling the Bronco back onto the dirt road. The number she'd read belonged to the clinic. Claire, her assistant, must have tried to reach her at the Glenn farm and been told she was on her way back to town. She listened for the beeper to go off again. Previously they'd set up a signal. One beep meant, "You're needed at the clinic." Two beeps meant, "Emergency—get to a phone fast." She eased her foot off the pedal when the beeper remained silent.

Within ten minutes, she'd parked and was rushing through the front door of the Mother's Clinic. Her eyes darted around the open area, searching for Claire but finding Annette O'Keefe, her husband, Johnny, and a man she'd never laid eyes on before. They were in the back of the room, taking Annette's blood pressure.

Slowing her pace, she crossed the room sedately. Rather than interrupt, she waited to be noticed.

"Did you see it?" Annette asked, pumping the rubber ball with one hand as she watched the gauge. "It sort of blips. Watch the needle."

"I don't see a thing," Johnny replied. "Look, sweetheart, I'll be responsible for weighing and measuring you, but you'll have to have Claire or Elaine check your blood pressure reading."

"You ought to have a nurse doing this," the stranger muttered under his breath.

Elaine stepped forward. All eyes turned toward her. She heard Johnny's sigh of relief and saw Annette's smile before she turned her eyes toward the stranger. "Why?"

"Because Annette doesn't know the first thing about practicing medicine. Until she started this natural childbirth nonsense she thought a thermometer was something you poked into raw meat to tell when it was done." Winking in Annette's direction, he added, "Not that a mere thermometer can keep her from burning dinner."

Elaine bristled, prepared to defend her patient. Annette laughed and punched the unidentified man in the ribs, saving Elaine from taking his razzing seriously.

"You must be Stuart," Elaine said, remembering Annette's comments about having an older brother who was an even bigger tease than her husband. She extended her hand and introduced herself. "Elaine Kramer, your sister's midwife."

Stuart did a double take as he looked at the young woman who confidently held out her hand. He'd mistakenly assumed she was another patient, which was reasonable enough, considering the fact that his sister had led him to believe Elaine Kramer was a cross between a kindly grandmother and a saint. As his dark eyes took in her trim figure, neither apple pies or angels' wings crossed his mind.

"Ms. Kramer," he responded, politely taking her hand. He hoped he'd concealed his astonishment, but one look at Annette's dimpled cheeks told him he hadn't fooled her. "You aren't exactly the way Annette described you."

"How's that?" Elaine asked. Annette's mischievous grin and her brother's I'll-get-you-later glare aroused her curiosity.

"Angelic." Annette supplied the answer with undisguised glee.

"Motherly. I distinctly remember one of you using that word," Stuart countered. "As in 'Fifty or older.'"

"Uh-uh," Johnny said. "I said Elaine would make a terrific godmother. Selective listening on your part, Stuart. Your preconceived notion that godmothers and grandmothers have to be the same age misled you."

"He's got a lot of erroneous preconceived notions," Elaine said good-naturedly, noting that her brother was still holding Elaine's hand. For the last couple of years she'd been trying to convince Stuart that it was time to stop playing mommy and daddy to her and start looking for a wife. In less than a minute he'd shown more interest in her midwife than in all the women she'd paraded in front of him put together. She hated to throw cold water on the definitely interested look she saw in his eyes, but this wasn't the time to play cupid. Later, Annette mused, hatching a plot even as she severed their handshake by saying, "That's why he's here."

"My brother-in-law thinks midwives are medical quacks," Johnny said. Then he added, "It's *Dr.* Cimarron."

The vixen and the rascal, Elaine mused, delighted by the good-natured banter. The supposed bombshell Johnny had dropped left her totally unscathed. She'd heard unfounded criticism too frequently to let it bother her.

Stuart felt an embarrassed flush tinge his face. "Talk about being misquoted," he muttered. Rallying, he added, "Good thing I'm not an attorney."

"Are you implying that I've committed slander?" Johnny asked incredulously. His china-blue eyes were round as he feigned complete innocence. "You *are* a doctor, and you did make quacking noises when we entered the clinic."

"Quack? Quack?" Annette jeered, obviously enjoying her brother's evident discomfort. To her way of thinking, each quack paid him back in full for his disparaging remarks about her cooking. Seeing his jaw drop was more rewarding than winning a blue ribbon at the state fair for her culinary expertise.

Elaine felt certain she must have gone to sleep without realizing it and fallen down the rabbit hole that led to the Mad Hatter's tea party. Stepping between Stuart and Annette, she raised her hands to quiet the family squabble. "Can I get a word in, please?"

Annette and her husband grinned, and Stuart's mouth opened, then snapped shut, giving Elaine the pause she needed. "Annette, why don't you and Johnny complete the workup on your chart while Dr. Cimarron and I go into my office for a private discussion, hmmm?"

Without further ceremony, Elaine turned toward the glass cubicle that overlooked the open area. The cushion chair behind her desk was a godsend, she thought as she took the pressure off her feet. Had she had the benefit of a solid eight hours' sleep, she might have tossed a few spicy remarks of her own into the droll family feud. Knowing two sleepless nights could change anybody's wit from spicy to acidic, she'd held her tongue.

What she didn't need at the moment was a heart-to-heart talk with Annette's overprotective brother. She'd have given anything to be able to prop her feet up on her desk and relax. Aware of the nagging pressure gathering between her shoulder blades, she realized this discussion had the potential of bringing on a king-size headache.

"I'm not a medical doctor," Stuart said, closing the door behind himself so they wouldn't be overheard. He'd always thought his sister had a somewhat off-the-wall sense of humor. Annette claimed it was a genetic quirk they both shared. While she'd been in his care, he'd carefully tried to discourage it, but Johnny encouraged it. Since she'd married Johnny—against his better judgment—and especially since she'd become pregnant, her humor had become more and more outrageous.

Quack, quack—humph! Those quacks gave credence to a theory he'd heard regarding the flow of blood changing during a woman's pregnancy—all of it went straight to the unborn child, and none of it reached the expectant mother's brain. Lack of oxygen made them say and do weird things.

Certain Elaine believed the charade the dynamic duo in the other room had performed, he stated unequivocally, "I don't perform operations, and I certainly don't make animal noises. I'm a dentist."

"Oh?" Elaine replied as a tingling sensation began at the base of her neck and advanced to her temples. The tingling changed to throbbing discomfort that coursed over the crown of her head. She propped her elbows on her desk and stroked her brow tenderly.

"Headache?"

Without giving his actions a second thought, Stuart moved behind her, saying, "My roommate in college was an aspiring chiropractor. Let's see if what he taught me will help."

She closed her eyes blissfully as his thumbs rotated slowly on her nape. Her head lolled to one side, then the other. A tiny soughing sound passed through her lips. In a voice that was louder than a whisper, she murmured, "I'll give you an hour to stop."

"You'd be asleep," he replied, noticing the sooty smudges beneath her long eyelashes. Tired and vulnerable, he thought, inching his thumbs up to the pressure points in her neck. And damned attractive.

Remembering the twinkle in his sister's eyes when she'd misled him about her midwife's age and appearance, he wondered what Annette was up to. Was she using reverse psychology?—you don't want to meet her, she's fat and fifty. Or had his lectures on matchmaking finally sunk into Annette's thick, mulish skull? Reformed matchmaker? Not likely, Stuart decided.

No, Annette weighed and measured her options as closely as she measured the ingredients of the prize-winning pies she baked. She'd wanted to avoid a confrontation between her "pigheaded" brother and the woman she'd come to admire more than she'd wanted to play cupid.

Stuart wondered if he'd mishandled the entire matter of Annette going to a midwife. The first time she'd said something about natural childbirth, he'd reacted like any other normal male—he'd been appalled. No doctor? No anesthetist? No emergency facilities? For a woman who fainted when she whacked her thumb with a hammer, the idea of giving birth at home was ludicrous. Still, he should have known Annette would be stubborn about it. Convinced he was getting nowhere fast, he'd casually mentioned that he'd like to meet this paragon, this living, breathing fairy godmother.

Now here he was doing one heck of a lot more than simply meeting her. As his thumbs followed the natural curve of her hairline, behind the dainty curve of her ears and up to her temples, his long fingers framed her uptilted face. Her dark hair brushed against his midsection, causing his stomach muscles to tighten.

Elaine watched him surreptitiously through her thick lashes. There was a vague family resemblance between Annette and her brother, but he reminded her of someone else, too. Who? she asked herself silently. The trite phrase used to describe every mysterious stranger fit Stuart perfectly: tall, dark and handsome. But there was a specific person, someone she saw regularly, someone in the medical profession who could have been a long-lost relative of Stuart's. She was too tired to think straight. Later, when those magical fingers of his weren't pushing all lucid thought from her mind, she'd remember.

"Better?" Stuart asked, leaning forward. Her eyes opened wider, clear of pain now. At first glance he'd thought they were emerald green. Close up, he realized they were blue. The golden flecks in them combined with the blue to make them look green. Blue emeralds, he mused whimsically, smiling.

"Immensely. Thanks."

It wasn't until he flashed her a perfect Hollywood smile that she realized who he looked like. The star of Claire's favorite medical soap opera. Claire never missed a second of the program, regardless of who was having a baby where. Elaine had often had to compete with the soap opera for Claire's attention when she wanted to leave an important message for a patient. No wonder Stuart seemed so familiar.

Stuart's hands lingered on her shoulder until he saw her tiny smile. Then he shoved them into his pants pockets. He was here to get Annette switched to a doctor, he thought, recalling his priorities.

Before he could broach the subject, Elaine said, "You don't like the idea of Annette having a midwife, right?"

"No, I don't."

"Why?"

"I want her to have the best." The answer slipped out of his mouth unaltered by tact. He half expected Elaine to jerk forward in her chair and read him the riot act. Instead, she leaned back in her chair and chuckled.

"By *best* I presume you mean an obstetrician and a hospital?"

He nodded. "I'm aware that Annette looks and acts like a sixties flower child. Thanks to Johnny's influence, she's going through a back-to-nature phase. Believe you me, that isn't how she was raised."

"Annette mentioned that your parents died during her early teens. You raised her."

The insight his sister had given her previously prepared Elaine for Stuart's next comment.

"Indulged is an accurate description. Until she got married, she thought every house came with a built-in microwave, vacuum system and housekeeper."

"You must be very proud of her," Elaine responded, suppressing the urge to smile. He made it sound as if Annette had gone from silks and satins to calico and gingham. "She's grown to be a charming, independent woman."

"Independent? Are you referring to her life-style? Frankly, I don't consider living in a log house out in the backwoods independent. Pioneer women went out of style at the turn of the century."

"Personally, I admire a person who can differentiate between life's necessities and frivolous luxuries."

Stuart wasn't aware he was pacing in front of her desk until she hit him with that statement. He stopped dead in his tracks. No woman who wasn't under the influence of a hippie husband who earned his living by playing with clay would prefer eking out a living to having everything her heart desired. Elaine must be pulling his leg.

He sat on the corner of her desk, pushing a stack of medical files out of the way. Those emerald-blue eyes of hers were sparkling with laughter. "You really think it's smart to be born with a silver spoon in your mouth and spit it out?"

"I can't argue with your logic." His smug nod made her rise to her feet so that he was no longer looking down on her and add, "However, I don't consider your sister's choice dumb."

"Neither do I. As I said, she's going through a phase. What scares the devil out of me is the strong possibility that she'll come out of that phase during labor. Pain does force a person into accepting reality. Stuck out in the boonies, miles from anywhere, what are you going to do if she panics?"

"She won't."

"You wouldn't care to put that in writing, would you?"

"I can't guarantee that she won't momentarily panic any more than you can guarantee that she'd be happier with the silver spoon." Elaine gestured toward the curtained area where she knew Annette and Johnny were busily taking measurements. "I can guarantee that she'll be prepared for delivery—a natural delivery—in her home, where she's chosen to have her baby. She won't be scared, or doped up, or in danger."

Her sincerity had Stuart wishing he agreed with her, but cold, hard facts didn't lie. He'd heard a doctor say that the most arduous journey a person made in his lifetime was through the birth canal. He didn't want anything to happen to Annette, and he sure as hell didn't want anything to happen to her baby.

Aware from the stubborn jut of his jaw that she hadn't swayed him an inch, Elaine raked her fingers through her hair, trying to find an argument within his range of experience. "Are your offices in a hospital?"

"No," Stuart replied, wondering where this new tactic of hers was leading. "They're in a professional building on the outskirts of Roanoke Rapids."

"Are some of your patients scared when they arrive?"

"I won't say my patients draw smiling faces when they enter their dental appointments on their calendars," he admitted. Driving home the difference between their chosen professions, he added, "But I haven't lost a patient yet."

"By 'lost' you don't mean to another dentist, do you?"

"No, I don't."

"Well, it should ease your mind to know that I haven't lost any patients, either, Doctor." She paused and looked him straight in the eye. "Do you always administer novocaine?"

"Only when necessary to keep my patient comfortable," he said, seeing the direction of her questions.

"Wouldn't it be better to hospitalize them and knock them out with novocaine or laughing gas?"

Elaine knew she'd made her point when Stuart's leg stopped swinging lazily and his foot lowered to the floor. In one fluid motion he was off the edge of her desk. His angelic grin was a duplicate of his sister's when she'd made duck noises.

"How 'bout a sledgehammer?" he asked irreverently. He motioned to an imaginary patient to come in and be seated, keeping one arm behind his back. "Mrs. Smith, please come in and be seated. You're here to have your teeth cleaned? Believe me, you won't feel a thing." His concealed hand arced downward. "Ker-thunk!"

Weary though she was, Elaine couldn't stop herself from chuckling as she watched Stuart dust off his hands as though he'd completed a job well done. "Annette came by her sense of humor honestly," she mused aloud.

"Uh-uh, Ms. Kramer," Stuart said, shaking his head. "I'll admit you've given me something to think about regarding the necessity of hospitalizing every woman who has a baby, but never in a million years will I admit that I was the role model for Annette's wacky sense of humor."

"'Quack' and 'ker-thunk' sound like brother and sister to me," she argued amiably. She glanced through the plate-glass window that separated her office from the open area. Annette and Johnny had completed her monthly checkup and were moving toward the office. Elaine pushed herself from her chair. "Let's agree to disagree on both subjects—Annette having a midwife, and the source of her sound effects, hmmm?"

"For the time being," Stuart agreed. His ready smile slipped when he added, "No negative influence on my part unless something out of the ordinary happens.''

"Should a problem arise, I have a medical doctor on standby for emergencies." Elaine extended her hand to seal the truce. Stuart took it and squeezed her fingers gently before reluctantly dropping her hand. "Thanks for caring enough to come and see me. Annette is lucky to have a husband and a brother who love her so much."

Annette overheard what Elaine said, and she beamed as she slipped one hand through the crook of Stuart's arm and the other through her husband's. "The two best men around these parts," she said, "and they are both part of the baby's family. Guess I am lucky."

Johnny handed Annette's chart to Elaine. "Good-news-bad-news time. Everything is normal, except her weight gain."

"How much?" Elaine asked as her eyes flickered over the check marks and numerical notations.

Annette groaned. "Three pounds."

Familiar with the dietary idiosyncrasies of pregnant women, Elaine asked, "Pickles-and-ice-cream cravings?"

"Popcorn and pickled beets," Johnny replied with a grimace.

"With butter and salt on the popcorn?" Elaine inquired. She watched Annette pinch her husband lightly. "Come on, Annette, 'fess up."

"A little light margarine and a sprinkling of salt."

"That's why the dairy farmers in Wisconsin are sending her personal thank-you notes," Johnny quipped, refusing to let his wife off the hook. "Don't worry, Elaine. I'll keep an eye on the popcorn kid."

Convinced Johnny would keep an eye on every morsel his wife put in her mouth, Elaine placed the chart on her desk, then glanced at Annette's ankles. Joint cooperation was important. Annette had to accept responsibility for watching her diet. "Pickling brine is salty, too. You're having a problem with swollen ankles, aren't you?"

"And fat feet," Annette answered, balancing on one foot and raising the other. After a small sigh and a wary glance at Stuart, she said, "Guess I'd better watch my salt intake, too."

Stuart reached for his billfold. "There's an old wive's tale about women losing a tooth for each child. Here's my business card."

"Isn't that just like a man," Annette said, ready to give her brother's nose a tweak. "Stuart comes in here to give you what for and leaves after he's given you his business card. Next thing I know, Johnny will be hauling samples of his pottery and showing them to you."

"Johnny doesn't have to hawk his wares," Elaine replied, flicking the corner of Stuart's card. "Johnny's reputation precedes him."

Johnny smiled smugly at his brother-in-law, as if to say, "See? I am good enough for your sister."

Sandwiched between two men she obviously loved dearly, Annette rolled her eyes heavenward. "Come on, you two rascals. Elaine's heard enough family feuding for one day."

"Bye," Elaine said, grinning as she watched Annette propel the two men, both of whom were twice her size, toward the door. "See you next month."

Stuart glanced over his shoulder and winked. Elaine had his business card. If Ms. Kramer was anything like the single women in Roanoke Rapids, he'd be hearing from her before his sister's next appointment. But when he saw her absentmindedly tuck the card in her pocket and acknowledge his wink with a tiny wave, he had second thoughts. Could it be that she wasn't like any woman he'd previously met?

Chapter Two

"See this tooth?" Margery Clements queried, stretching her lower lip and pointing to a back molar. "Must be abscessed. It's driving me crazy."

"I don't see any swelling. Did you call Dr. Richardson for an appointment?"

Elaine added "toothache" to the long list of minor problems in Margery's file. In the five months Margery had been a patient, her complaints had ranged from headaches to cramps in her big toe. Elaine suspected the cause was psychological rather than medical.

"He's on vacation," Elaine answered herself, recalling that the dentist had let her know he was going away.

"Humph! Tom says the doctors and dentists around here spend more time fishin' than he does."

"Annette O'Keefe's brother is a dentist in Roanoke Rapids." Within weeks of moving to Tyler, Elaine had discovered that being related to someone in town automatically served as a good reference. Everybody was related to somebody who could "fix ya up jist fine."

"Johnny O'Keefe's wife's brother?" Mulling over the family relationship and recalling the gossip Johnny had caused by marrying an outsider, Margery said, "I've seen her at the church gatherings. Annette sure is a cute little thing. Now that she's in the family way, every woman in town envies how Johnny cossets her. Course, it was a real shame he didn't marry Anne Marie Peterson. Months after Johnny got hitched, I saw poor little Anne Marie pining away in front of the store he used to rent to display his pottery. Her mother told me..."

Elaine nodded, only half listening to Margery's gossip, as she turned the knob on her Rolodex file. She copied Stuart's name and number on a slip of paper and handed it to Margery when she paused to take a breath. "I thought I remembered him giving me one of his business cards. Why don't you call Dr. Cimarron's receptionist to see if he can work you into his schedule immediately?"

"Dr. Stuart Cimarron," Margery said, reading from the paper Elaine had given her. "Dentist. You say he's Johnny O'Keefe's brother-in-law?"

"Uh-huh."

"Is he young?"

"Fairly. I'd say he's about your age—early thirties."

Margery tugged at the hem of the too-short polyester maternity top that stretched across her rounded midriff. "Gentle?"

"He seemed concerned about Annette's welfare." That's putting it mildly, Elaine thought. Any brother who bothered to personally visit his sister's midwife was exceptionally devoted. She rubbed the back of her neck, remembering how soothing his hands had been, how he'd relieved her tension headache within minutes of touching her. "Yes, I'd say he's gentle."

"I'll call him when I get home. Tom doesn't cotton to me going into the city to get things done, but maybe he won't object too much when I tell him Dr. Cimarron is Johnny's relative."

"I'm sure he'll take good care of you."

Margery braced her hands on the arms of the chair and heaved herself to her feet. She was seven months into her pregnancy, and her walk resembled a duck's waddle—feet pointed to the side, each step covering scant inches. "Two months to go," she complained. "I can't hear two heartbeats through that stethoscope thingamajig of yours, but I swear I feel like I'm carryin' twins. Maybe triplets."

Elaine mentally measured the width of the doorway and waited until Margery had gone through it before putting her arm over her shoulder and giving her an affectionate hug. Despite her moaning and groaning and her fondness for gossip, Elaine truly cared about Margery.

"You're doing fine. Don't forget the Lamaze class next week."

Margery stopped, and her gaze flitted around the room, landing everywhere but on Elaine's face. "You're sure Tom has to be here?"

"Positive. He's the person you want to be your coach during labor, isn't he?"

"Of course I want him to be there, but that doesn't mean it's where *he* wants to be. You know how squeamish men can be."

"Tom will be a big help on D day. But he has to learn the technique." She noticed Margery massaging the small of her back. "One of the first things he learns how to do is give a back rub."

"I can't picture Tom rubbing my back. He sort of feels like once he gets me pregnant I'm supposed to take care of everything by myself."

"Margery—" Elaine framed her patient's face with both hands until their eyes met "—he's the baby's father. He may not be the kind of man who can tell you how proud he is of you, but I'm certain that deep in his heart he is."

Straightening her shoulders, Margery smiled weakly. "It's a nice thought, Elaine. Sometimes I think he'd pay more attention to me if I grew scales and breathed water."

"Fishing is a hobby. You're his wife—the mother of his children. He must be proud of you."

"I suppose so," Margery conceded. "I guess after bein' married twelve years a man forgets how to sweet-talk. I'm not gripin', mind you. Tom's a good provider for me and the kids. He don't drink or carouse like some men do. Guess I oughta count my blessings. I wouldn't have Celeste and Sally if I didn't have him."

She put a protective hand on her rounded abdomen. "And I wouldn't have this sweet baby, either."

Listening to Margery rationalize Tom's benign neglect twisted Elaine's heart. Tom furnished Margery with food for the table, but emotionally he starved her. Having been on a emotional starvation diet herself during the last year of her marriage, Elaine could empathize.

"Tomorrow I want you to stand in front of the mirror and say, 'Margery, you look great. You feel great. Your family loves you.' Positive thinking. Keep working on it."

"I have. Tom nearly busted a gut laughin' when he heard me talkin' to myself. He says I'm gettin' crazy as a shad swimmin' in circles." She fussed with her hair with housework-roughened hands. Borrowing a teensy bit of Elaine's gumption, she said, "Maybe while I'm on the phone callin' Dr. Cimarron, I'll call Maisie at the beauty shop and make an appointment there, too."

"If it'll help you feel good about yourself, I'm all for it," Elaine said, encouraging the feeble thread of optimism in Margery's voice. "You take care of yourself. I'll look forward to seeing your new hairstyle at the Wednesday-night meeting."

After Margery left the clinic Elaine stood at the front window, marveling at how different a pregnancy could be, depending on what role the husband played. Annette glowed with an inner radiance; Margery trudged under her burden. Why the difference? The answer was simple: Johnny and Tom had different perspectives on fatherhood.

Johnny felt the baby was something wonderful he and Annette had created, a product of their love. Like the pottery he crafted, their child would be unique. With that in mind, Johnny was considerate, sympathetic and helpful.

Tom thought of his unborn child as one more mouth to feed, one more child competing for his wife's time and affection, one more voice to shout over. And yet, judging from the comments Margery had made, he refused to take the responsibility for preventing her from getting pregnant. It didn't make sense.

Why couldn't the Toms of the world understand how important loving support was during a pregnancy? They weren't blind. They had to see the physical changes taking place. To Elaine's way of thinking, if there was one time in a woman's life when a wife should be put on a pedestal, it was during pregnancy.

During Tom's one and only visit to the Mother's Clinic, Elaine had let him know her opinion. He'd responded by slapping his knee and guffawing as though she'd told a hilarious traveling-salesman-farmer's-daughter joke. Then, as though trying to top her, he'd told her that it would take a heavy-duty crane to get Margery up on a pedestal—and then she'd squash it, unless it was made of reinforced concrete. Neither Elaine nor Margery had found that humorous.

When he'd managed to reduce his laughter to the level of a snicker, he'd told Elaine in no uncertain terms that women had been put on this earth to have babies and tend to their menfolk. The only reason a man and woman raised a passel of kids was so they'd have help with the farm chores and somebody to support them in their old age. And furthermore, he'd concluded irately, he was "too busy" feeding hungry mouths to be bothered with "women's stuff."

Half-moon imprints on the palms of Elaine's hands, caused by her short fingernails, were the price she'd paid for remaining calm during his tirade. Knowing it was pointless to confuse Tom with logic, she'd held her tongue. His mind was already made up, and she'd be wasting her breath. She'd politely informed him of the clinic's policy of having the husband coach his wife during delivery.

"No big deal," he'd replied, "I was raised on a farm. Delivering a baby can't be much different than calving."

Since then, Elaine had tried to provide the emotional support Margery needed. Each visit to the clinic ended with a pep talk, a lesson in positive thinking. Sadly, Margery's once-a-month appointments at the clinic and Elaine's phone calls weren't enough to sustain her. Tom had daily input. Margery believed everything Tom said was the gospel truth.

Elaine watched Margery cross the street and enter Compton's dress shop. Elaine knew Margery would leave the shop empty-handed. Tom regularly berated Margery for her dowdy appearance, but he kept a tight grip on the family purse strings. For Margery to spend his "hard-earned money" getting "gussied up" was pure selfishness. The chances of Margery buying a new maternity dress or making a hair appointment and keeping it were slim to none if Tom got wind of her plans.

Mystified by Tom's illogical behavior and Margery's lack of backbone, Elaine shook her head. It was pointless to continue knocking her head against a stone wall worrying about Margery's marital situation. She couldn't change Tom's attitudes any more than she'd been able to change her ex-husband's. She hated to admit it, but some things in life seemed static, they couldn't be altered by good intentions or counseling. But Elaine knew she'd keep trying. It was part of her job. Margery's mental health during her pregnancy was as important as her physical health.

Arriving at work, Claire Johnson waved as she crossed in front of the window. Elaine's attention was drawn away from Margery's problems. No one could look at Claire for two seconds without returning her infectious smile. She was dressed casually in bright pink slacks and a pink-and-white striped blouse, an outfit that matched her vivacious personality. Her short, curly brown hair bounced with each jaunty, long-legged step she took. There wasn't a shy bone in Claire's body or a repressed thought in her mind. What Claire thought, she said. Elaine didn't mind Claire's outspokenness, and she thanked her lucky stars for having bumped into Claire while she'd been selecting wallpaper for the clinic. They'd become the best of friends, as well as co-workers. Claire appeared flighty, but underneath her moptop hairstyle there was an astute woman who was a stickler for detail.

"Hey, boss lady, how's it going?" Claire breezed through the door, swinging her purse and snapping the bubble gum that seemed to be a permanent fixture in her mouth. Without waiting for a reply, she shifted her gum to the other side of her mouth and said, "I saw Margery getting into her pick-em-up truck. She looked pleased as a kid getting a slice of ice-cold watermelon at the Fourth of July picnic when I gave her the maternity clothes you'd loaned Mrs. Glenn." Snap. "Margery's old man will probably pitch a fit. He was valedictorian of the class when he graduated from the poor-but-proud school. Wouldn't surprise me if he cut those smocks into pieces and mailed them back to you."

Elaine waited for Claire to take a quick breath. "I'd be surprised if Tom notices what she's wearing."

"You're probably right." Snap. "Say, Margery said you recommended Johnny O'Keefe's brother-in-law to fix her teeth." Snap. "You didn't tell me you'd switched dentists. Not that I'd blame you. One of Purity Mason's kids told my sister Lucy that Doc Richardson pulled her baby tooth with a string. Charged Purity five dollars for the office visit, too. Do you believe that?"

Before Claire could snap her gum, signaling another change of topic, Elaine interrupted her. "Dr. Richardson is on vacation. That's why I suggested Margery call Stuart."

"Stuart, hmmm?" Claire raised an eyebrow speculatively. "Before Pete and I started dating, I met *Dr. Cimarron* at one of Johnny's pottery shows. Needless to say, we didn't get to a first-name basis—not for lack of trying on my part. At the time, I thought he seemed interested enough to call me. He didn't, so I called him. He was polite but busy. Lord have mercy, between his work schedule and his social calendar he must be busier than ants on an open honey jar." Snap. Her eyes shone with curiosity. "So start at the beginning and tell me all the lurid details. Who called whom?"

"No calls. No lurid details." Elaine ignored Claire's exasperated sigh. With businesslike briskness, she began straightening the magazines on the end table next to the sofa. "Don't you remember my telling you about Annette and Johnny bringing Stuart to the clinic?"

From the sly glance Claire shot in her direction, Elaine knew she'd failed in her attempt to appear nonchalant. Her hands fluttered along the seams of her pants. Knowing the best defense was a good offense, she said, "You'd better get rid of your gum before the next patient arrives. Your snap-crackle-and-pop is enough to bring on labor pains."

"Now that you mention it, I do recall your commenting on Annette bringing her brother in for a short visit. Didn't you say he was upset about Annette's decision to have her baby at home?" Claire removed a tissue from her purse and disposed of the gum. "What else did you discuss to get friendly enough to be on a first-name basis?"

"Nothing."

Claire grinned. Something had happened while Stuart had been there, or Elaine wouldn't be fussing with the collar of her blouse, refusing to look her in the eye. "Now I know you're hiding something. Lucy ducks her head and denies everything when she's lying through her teeth, too."

Giving in to the temptation to make up a story that would make Claire's soap operas seem tame, Elaine whispered, "He gave me a massage."

"A massage?" Claire squeaked. "As in him putting his hands on your body?"

"Yep." Elaine glanced at her watch, then strolled toward her office. To hint at juicy information, then stop short of divulging all the details, was enough to drive Claire totally bonkers. "You're going to miss your soap opera if you don't get busy."

Claire was obviously torn between her daily dose of television drama and the possibility of real-life drama taking place right there at the clinic, and her head swiveled from the television to Elaine's retreating back. "I could have sworn you didn't have an ornery streak until today. So help me, boss lady, I can see a mile-wide streak running right up between your shoulder blades. You can't tell me a stranger gave you a massage and walk away as though having a man's hands touching those curves of yours is a daily occurrence!"

"Sure I can," Elaine responded flippantly. "There's nothing else to tell."

Claire smacked her forehead with her hand. "Lord! What is it? Don't you trust me?"

"Completely."

To encourage Elaine to confide in her, Claire defended her ability to keep a secret. "You know I'm the only person in Tyler who knows you've been married. I kept that secret, didn't I?"

"Claire, I trust you implicitly. There simply isn't anything else to tell."

"You wouldn't lie to me, would you? I mean, I've told you all the glorious details about meeting and falling in love with Pete."

Elaine crossed her heart and raised her hand in a gesture Claire readily understood. "Tease you? Guilty. Lie to you? Never." Elaine knew Claire would never forgive her if she missed an episode of her favorite program. Better to tell the whole truth, she decided, than to listen to Claire moan and groan for the remainder of the day. "Stuart was here the morning the Glenns' baby was born. Remember? I hadn't slept for forty-eight hours. He must have realized I had a throbbing headache, so he massaged my neck. As he left he gave me his business card, which I filed in the Rolodex. I haven't heard from him since then. End of the exciting adventure of Dr. Cimarron's visit to his sister's midwife."

"Oh, Elaine." Exasperation dripped from both words. "Aren't you the least bit interested in him?"

"He seemed like a nice guy."

"Nice guy! Nice guy?" Claire repeated as though she couldn't believe her boss's attitude. She held her palms up for Elaine's inspection. "Nice guys don't make my hands sweat just by hearing their names mentioned."

"This is the woman who's engaged to the local heartthrob speaking? What happened to all the *ooh*-ing and *aah*ing I normally hear when Pete's name is mentioned?"

"I love Pete, but Dr. Cimarron could be a stand-in for my favorite doctor on the soaps. You know, the one whose wife may have murdered her first husband.''

Elaine grinned. "You're right. He does resemble that actor. I noticed it, too."

"Did you call Dr. Cimarron?" Claire sashayed into the glass enclosure and plopped down on the vinyl couch. "What'd he say?"

"Why would I phone him? Dr. Richardson gave me a six-month dental checkup in March."

"You're kidding me again, aren't you?"

Elaine shook her head. "No. I didn't have any reason to call Stuart."

"Good grief! You have to have a legitimate reason to make one piddly phone call that could change the course of your life? Dr. Cimarron gives you his phone number and you don't call him? You're hopeless."

"I'm certain Stuart didn't give me his business card for social purposes. Besides—" Elaine shrugged her shoulders "—I gave up chasing boys in the third grade. Too many skinned knees, and too few boyfriends."

"Calling a man isn't considered chasing nowadays. It's expressing your equality, letting him know you're assertive—a woman of the eighties."

"Making a phone call doesn't prove any of those things." Picking up a current medical magazine Elaine flipped through it, hoping Claire would get the idea that they'd thoroughly covered the topic of conversation. "There's an interesting article in here that I want you to read. A pediatrician in St. Louis has done a study on factors that influence right- or left-handedness. He says an infant lying in his crib rolls toward the light and reaches for it. So if the baby is lying on his left side he reaches with his right hand."

"I guess the Cimarron case is closed due to your old-fashioned ideas?" Claire asked, finally taking the hint.

"So if a mother changes the placement of the crib—"

"Okay. I give up." Succumbing to the fact that she couldn't prod her friend into calling Stuart, Claire raked the scattered file folders on Elaine's desk into a pile, picked them up and marched toward the door. "Just remember. When you're a lonely little old lady, don't blame it on me. I tried. You were just too stubborn to cooperate."

"...the child can develop his coordination on both sides of his body." Elaine completed what she'd being saying as though Claire had been listening. "Interesting, huh?"

"Titillating," Claire replied sarcastically, rolling her eyes. "Want to know something that really boggles my mind? Your lack of interest in the male species. It makes me wonder if you think sex without impregnation is a waste of time. At other times I wonder if you're still yearning for your ex-husband. One thing for sure, you're absolutely the only woman in five counties who has Stuart Cimarron's phone number and hasn't dialed it."

Elaine watched Claire over the top of the magazine as she pointed toward her head, made a circle with her finger, then pointed at her.

Crazy? Uh-uh, Elaine mused. Sane. Cautious. Claire considered herself an expert on affairs of the

heart, but she hadn't been hurt. Elaine had. She'd
given her love once, completely, freely, without res-
ervation, and had it tossed back in her face. Until
Claire understood that love could cause as much sorrow as joy, she'd just have to go on wondering how
Elaine could let her head govern her heart.

Stuart read Margery's information card with undisguised interest. "Ms. Kramer recommended me?"

"Our local dentist is on vacation." Margery settled
into the black leather chair and laced her fingers together on her rounded stomach. "He's always away
when you need him."

"Hmmm," Stuart responded, too ethical to encourage disparaging remarks about a colleague in another town. "What seems to be your problem?"

"This tooth back here." She opened wide and
pointed to a back molar. "It's okay during the day,
but at night it feels like someone stuck a firecracker
back there."

Stuart lowered the overhead examination light into
position. His assistant, June Lawrence, handed him
the highly polished stainless steel tool he needed to see
the inside of Margery's mouth.

Aware of the fear in her eyes, he smiled reassuringly, then asked, "How far along are you?"

"Seven months."

June handed him a small pick as he contemplated
the necessity of taking X rays, considering the possible risk to the fetus.

"Firstborn?"

"Third. Two girls—Celeste is six and Sally is three. Tom says this one had better be a boy."

"Tom. Your husband?"

"Yeah." By way of explanation, Margery added, "Girls aren't much help with the heavy chores around the farm."

"This shouldn't hurt," he said, observing Margery's fingers clenching together when she saw another instrument passed to him. "I'm just going to take a look. Then we'll decide what needs to be done."

Deciding X rays were out, Stuart lightly ran the pick between the gum and the tooth she'd pointed to. There it was. A small dark spot indicating the early stages of decay, right beneath the gum line. "Tell me if this hurts."

"You gonna have to pull it?" Margery asked when he'd removed his fingers from her mouth and quietly murmured a number and some other things she didn't understand to his assistant.

"No. A small filling should do nicely."

Margery took several deep breaths. "Deep-breathing exercise. Elaine told me to do this when I get overexcited or nervous. Works most of the time."

While June got the supplies he needed to fill the cavity, Stuart used his own technique to get his patient relaxed—charm.

"I've heard about pregnant women having a special inner glow and thought it was a bunch of hogwash, but looking at you and my sister proves me wrong. Both of you have a similar Mona Lisa smile."

"Thanks, Doc. Elaine says it's because we are special."

"Did you have your children at home?" The thought of Annette having her child without adequate medical supervision continued to bother him, despite his respect for Elaine. Childbirth was a mystery to a man. Perhaps talking to a woman who's had her child at home would give him additional reassurance.

"Heck, no. Tom was workin' for a construction company that had insurance benefits. With my first daughter, Celeste, we were both young and scared. After Sally came along, he sorta took it for granted that havin' a baby was easier than fallin' off a log. When I got pregnant this time, Tom had heard about my neighbor down the road a piece having her child natural, at home. No muss, no fuss, says my Tom." Margery lifted one shoulder in a gesture that said, "Who am I to argue with my husband?"

"So you went to the Mother's Clinic?"

"Yep. At first I was kinda leery. You know, with Elaine being new to Tyler. No relatives there or anything. But she's been welcomed into town like a free bale of alfalfa delivered to a stable."

Stuart grinned at Margery's choice of words. Elaine didn't remind him of a cumbersome bale wrapped in wire. No indeed. At odd moments during the past couple of weeks, he'd caught himself staring out his office window, wondering about a certain attractive lady with languorous blue-green eyes and silky dark hair. While he'd stroked her neck she'd been decidedly touchable, nothing at all like alfalfa.

He must have antagonized her more than he'd realized, he mused, or else she'd have contacted him.

He tried to convince himself that Elaine had sent Margery as a go-between because she hadn't wanted to make direct contact. Hard as he'd tried, though, he couldn't convince himself that Elaine had given him a second thought.

You're spoiled, buddy, he told himself silently. You're beginning to believe what your office staff says about you: single, attractive and available. And popular, too, judging by the number of dinner invitations he turned down each week. That wasn't conceit or arrogance; it was fact.

He liked female companionship. Why sit at home alone when some sweet woman wanted to spend time with him? Only a fool wouldn't take advantage of what had always been in ready supply.

That wasn't to say he filled his empty hours exclusively with females. Occasionally he'd get together with "the boys," but the majority of the guys his age were married with kids. Careers, wives and children took priority over poker games and fishing expeditions. Until the past year or so his buddies had envied him. Now Stuart had the nagging suspicion that he was the one missing out on something, something he hadn't experienced in the string of casual relationships he'd had since Annette had married Johnny.

"Doctor?" While he'd been woolgathering, Margery had become increasingly fidgety. "You aren't going to knock me out to fill the tooth, are you?"

Recalling his conversation with Elaine, he grinned and shook his head. "The cavity is shallow. I don't think we'll need novocaine unless the nerve is exposed."

"I hate shots. Numbs half of my tongue. Can't talk or eat or anything. Elaine says a strong mind can control physical discomfort."

Tom says, Elaine says... Stuart wondered if Margery had a single original thought she could call her own, to say nothing of the willpower to control pain. "You tell me if you're uncomfortable. There's no reason to suffer needlessly."

He'd said exactly the same words to Annette when they'd discussed childbirth. What was it about the women who went to the Mother's Clinic? Somehow or other, Elaine Kramer changed them into superwomen.

"Positive thinking is better than painkillers," Margery told him. "Save your shots for someone who needs them."

June returned, carrying a tray with the necessary materials. As he worked, Stuart watched for any sign of pain: flinching, jaw locking, frowning. He hummed a tune from Bob York's latest album as he worked. Margery breathed deeply a few times but otherwise remained calm.

"That does it." Raising the light and the back of the dental chair, he added, "Elaine would be proud of you if she'd been here."

Margery basked in the glow of his praise. "Didn't hurt a bit. Elaine's a good teacher." She straightened her smock and grinned. "Next time I'm out at Johnny's I'll tell your sister what a great dentist she has in the family."

"I appreciate the vote of confidence—especially with my sister. If you have any other problems while Dr. Richardson is away, just call me."

Long after Margery had left his office, after he'd finished with his appointments for the day, Stuart contemplated his standard procedure of thanking another medical person for a referral. Usually he'd have his receptionist send a thank-you card. If the opportunity presented itself, he'd return the favor by putting in a good word for the doctor. None of the regular procedures seemed appropriate for Elaine.

Roanoke Rapids was only a half-hour drive from Tyler, he mused, recalling Annette's dinner invitation. He'd pass right through Tyler on the way to his sister's lake house. Since he'd be in the neighborhood anyway, why not stop by the clinic and thank Elaine personally? Stuart grinned at the simple solution.

He stripped off his white jacket, suddenly anxious to be on his way. Humming aloud, he locked up his office and crossed the parking lot to his Mercedes.

June weather in Roanoke Rapids tended to be hot and sultry. Stuart didn't mind. He lowered the top on his car and started the engine.

When he was outside of town he goosed the gas pedal, thoroughly enjoying the surge of power, the feel of the late-afternoon sunshine, the smells of summer. Wind whipped his hair into careless disarray. He didn't notice or care. He was anticipating spending the evening with Elaine.

Whoa, fella. He was getting ahead of himself. His original purpose had been to drop by the clinic on his way to Annette's and thank Elaine for sending him a patient. Still, the idea of getting to know her was appealing. It wasn't just the fact that she was easy on the eyes. They had common interests, too: medicine and Annette.

Eyes, he mused, remembering the unusual color of Elaine's eyes. Blue irises with flashing yellow flecks that made them appear green. Fascinating eyes that could melt a man's resolution and change his attitudes. She'd challenged his beliefs, then convinced him to reconsider his position. Persuasive, sincere eyes that had worked their magic on her clients as well as on him. The eyes, like the woman, were unusual—and intriguing.

Lost in thought, he arrived in Tyler in what seemed like seconds. He pulled in front of the Mother's Clinic and parked. The interior lights were on. Someone was there. As he moved toward the door, he silently sent up a prayer that the stork wouldn't be arriving this evening.

Elaine felt a gust of hot, humid air as the door opened. Reflexively she peeked through the small slit in the drapery enclosure to see who'd arrived. Her hand almost dropped the stethoscope she'd placed on Cristy Baker's stomach. Cristy was in her fourth month of pregnancy, and she was enthralled by the sound of her child's heartbeat. Unexpectedly seeing Stuart had made Elaine's own heart rate lurch in surprise.

"Dr. Cimarron, come in," she said cordially, parting the drapes to talk to him. "Have a seat and I'll be with you in a moment. We're almost finished."

Knowing that only a cotton curtain separated the privacy of the examining room from the area where Stuart had taken a seat, she drew upon her powers of concentration to give Cristy her undivided attention. The last thing she wanted was a confrontation with Stuart because she'd been too distracted to do her job.

"What am I going to do about my heartburn?" Cristy asked, her voice lowered. She removed the stethoscope from her ears. "I swear, all I'm hearing are air bubbles swimming from my stomach to my heart."

"How many sodas do you drink each day?" Elaine had noticed that Cristy's second stop when she'd arrived at the clinic—the first had been the washroom—had been at the soda machine. Elaine appreciated the need for a cool, bubbling drink in this weather, but she also was aware of the side effects.

"Four. Maybe five, but they're diet sodas."

"Hot tea." Cristy fanned her face in response. Elaine nodded in agreement. Brewed drinks were unappealing in hot, sticky weather. "Refrigerate a bottle of tea. No ice. Keep your meals small but frequent. You might try chewing gum. Sometimes that helps."

"From leg cramps to heartburn in less than a month." Cristy groaned. "You're certain I'm progressing nicely?"

"Absolutely. Once you stopped tiptoeing around to keep from waking Bob and started taking the calcium supplement, the leg cramps went away, didn't they?"

"Yeah. Bob was a real sweetheart. His night-duty shift ended last week."

"Trust me. Your weight gain was less than two pounds."

"I'm not starving myself or the baby. I'm walking a mile a day." Her hand gestured in a motion like a feather on gigantic waves. "Up the hill, down the hill, over the hill, around the hill, thinking lovely thoughts, singing silly songs."

Grinning, Elaine caught her hand and squeezed her fingers. "You're doing great. Keep up the good work."

Stuart listened to the soft voices coming from behind the curtain. Elaine's confidence, knowledge and enthusiasm were just what an anxiety-ridden expectant mother needed. Nothing seemed beyond her capabilities.

When she parted the drapes, Stuart took a breath worthy of Margery's relaxation exercise. A sweet tingle circled his heart. How could anyone who looked so beautiful sound so professional? Today she wasn't tired and rumpled. She wore a trendy jungle-print shirt and double-pleated khaki slacks. Small gold hoop earrings dangled from her earlobes. Her hair capped her head in soft, inviting curls. His fingers itched to touch it.

Reality was decidedly better than his frequent daydreams, he thought as Elaine introduced Cristy. The twin lines etched between her brows were gone. She looked—he struggled to find a suitable adjective—deliciously fresh.

"Nice to meet you, Cristy," he said automatically, his eyes still on Elaine. He didn't hear Cristy's nervous twitter or see her speculative glance at Elaine.

"Well, I've got to run." Cristy excused herself and crossed to the door. "Bob's probably waiting for dinner."

"Bye," Elaine said, barely loud enough to be heard.

Silently clearing his throat, Stuart said, "Margery's tooth is fixed. Thanks for thinking of me."

"Margery called yesterday. She said your receptionist had set up an emergency appointment." Smiling, she said teasingly, "I didn't know dentists had emergencies. Next thing I know I'll be in the bedroom delivering a baby and you'll be in the living room making a house call on another member of the family."

Far less ruffled by what Elaine had said than by watching her lips form the words, he murmured, "I'm on my way to make a house call now."

"Really?"

"Hmmm. Care to ride along and watch me work?"

The mere thought of riding anywhere with him made breathing difficult. "I have a previous engagement."

Stuart silently berated himself. Of course. It's Friday night, you clodhopper. Deciding to check out the competition, he asked, "A date? Someone you're serious about?"

Amazed by the personal nature of his question, Elaine was at a loss for words. She began thinking about where she'd been invited to spend the evening. She started adding one and one together and came up with a cupid in the woodpile. "A patient invited me over for dinner."

"That patient wouldn't happen to be my sister, would it?" Before she could answer, Stuart added, "The same sister whose voice was quivering with excitement when she invited her brother to dinner?"

Elaine nodded. "Sometimes my patients think a midwife should have a husband and a flock of kids waiting at home. When I don't live up to their expectations they get this uncontrollable urge to rectify that situation. I'll call Annette and make some excuse."

"And spoil her evening? Uh-uh. She's probably at home keeping one eye on the oven while she oils up the shotgun. You aren't the first woman my sister and her charming husband have paraded under my nose. Definitely the loveliest, mind you, but not the first." He tapped the side of his face with the tip of his index finger as he thought of ways to twist his sister's plot. "Annette has a fit when I interfere in her life. It's only fair that I—"

"Stop. The last time you were here I saw how you and your sister tease each other—charred meat and quack, quacks, remember?" The devilish twinkle lighting his dark eyes confirmed that he did. "Annette is my patient. I can't—"

Stuart took her by the arm, led her to the couch and sat down close beside her, and she was no longer certain what she could and couldn't do.

"Come to think of it, I'll bet my little sister had something up her sleeve when she loudly protested against my saying I'd like to talk you," he mused aloud. In reply to her shaking her head in silent refusal, he said, "It's after hours."

"I'm on call twenty-four hours a day." She patted the beeper hanging from her belt for emphasis. "I'm a professional. I can't pull a practical joke on a patient, even if she is your sister."

"You won't have to. I'll do all the talking. You just sit there looking gorgeous and I'll deflect the arrows cupid's little helper—namely my sister—shoots in our direction."

The electrifying combination of Stuart's smile and his hand, which was still on her arm, short-circuited her resistance. Convinced his protectiveness toward his sister would keep him from saying or doing anything scandalous, she nodded.

Stuart dropped her arm and rubbed his hands together in anticipation. "By the end of the evening, Annette will be absolutely thrilled with the success of her ploy to find a suitable woman for her one and only brother."

"You sister is a bright woman. If what you're planning is based on the premise that you met and instantaneously fell in love with me, I seriously doubt that Annette will fall for it."

Stuart gave her a cocky wink as he pushed the door open. "Annette will believe what she wants to believe. By midnight she'll be humming the wedding march and ringing church bells."

Chapter Three

Stuart took the black medical bag from her hand, put it behind the passenger seat and helped Elaine into the Mercedes.

"Like it?" he asked when he saw her glance appreciatively at the calfskin upholstery.

Sleek and sporty—like its owner, Elaine thought, nodding. "Are you certain it wouldn't be better for me to follow you in my own car? Sometimes I do have to make emergency calls."

"Nonsense," he replied, crossing to his side of the car. "Do you want me to put the top up?"

"No, thanks." Elaine anticipated feeling the wind capriciously blowing her hair as she felt the fine texture of the leather upholstery. The seats in her car were covered with vinyl. Mentally comparing their cars she realized her income was a mere pittance compared to his. She shrugged and placed her hand in her lap, dismissing the thought. She'd enjoy the pleasure of riding with Stuart, regardless of what kind of vehicle he drove.

The car's engine roared obediently when Stuart turned the key. "I waited years to own this little baby. After Annette got married, I could afford one without starving to death."

"Annette mentioned that you'd raised her." Her eyes twinkled, bright and shiny as a wet leaf, as she said teasingly, "Actually, I believe her exact words had something to do with you bulldozing her around."

"I may have tried," he admitted, grinning, "but no one bulldozes Annette. Her choosing you rather than the ob-gyn that I recommended is a perfect example of how she listens, smiles, then does as she damned well pleases."

"Annette dislikes interference of any sort, be it from her big brother or a doctor."

"The last time I talked to her on the telephone she quoted statistics on the rate of intervention in hospital deliveries. Having gone through medical training myself, I can understand how a doctor who's been trained in a fast-paced environment would be tempted to hurry up Mother Nature's slow pace."

"In some hospitals the chances of a woman's delivery being speeded up by a drug are one in three."

"My sister quoted the same statistic," he replied dryly. Elaine must have supplied his sister with ammunition for their common cause. He took his eyes off the road and glanced at Elaine for confirmation.

What he saw made his heart skip a beat. Her face was lifted toward the sun, her eyes closed, her lips slightly parted, as though she were waiting for a lover's kiss. Silky strands of hair whipped across her cheeks in wild abandon. When she raised her hand and let her fingers splay through her hair, fluffing it, the sight of her blouse cupping the lush fullness of her breasts almost caused him to miss a curve in the highway.

"Annette asked for facts and figures," Elaine said. She didn't mind his knowing where Annette had obtained her information. "I thought you were glad she'd chosen me as a midwife."

"I am." Increasingly glad, Stuart mused, thinking more of his appreciation of her as a woman than of her professional qualifications. "But I still have reservations. That's partially due to knowing how my sister picks a cause, then tries to convince the world she's right. The midwives of America are her current favorite. She'd close the maternity wards in hospitals across the nation if she had her way. I'm receptive to her ideas, but not to that extent."

Elaine gave a small sigh. She felt contented and annoyed at the same time. She'd responded to his comments rationally, but convincing Stuart of the validity of her profession wasn't the immediate problem. Annette's delivery of her child was several months away. While Elaine had been making appropriate comments, in the back of her mind she'd been wondering exactly what sort of devilish plans he'd made to counter Annette's attempt to play matchmaker. Discovering his strategy was only minutes away.

His pretending to dislike her intensely would be the most effective, she decided, frowning. The thought of spending the evening thwarting his verbal thrusts lacked appeal.

Stuart saw Elaine grimace. Did she expect, after one short conversation, to have changed his mind completely? She was breathtaking, true, but his brain wasn't suffering from oxygen starvation.

"Annette isn't the only one in the family who can quote statistics. Ninety-nine percent of American women deliver their babies in hospitals. Four out of five of those babies are delivered by obstetricians. All those other women can't be wrong."

Elaine slowly opened her eyes and turned her head toward Stuart. Was he starting early, picking a fight before they even arrived at his sister's house? He'd certainly chosen the right topic. She didn't consider herself oversensitive, but she had strong views regarding her chosen occupation.

"I thought your primary concern was for the safety of Annette and her baby," she replied dryly. "The mortality rate of newborns in the United States ranks ninth worldwide. In seven out of the eight *safest* countries, most of the women are attended by midwives."

Knowing he'd struck a raw nerve, he paused. He had the distinct feeling that her pleasant tone and relaxed pose were deceptive. If he dared to probe further, he'd most likely find a tigress ready to pounce. And dissension between them would spoil his plans. Annette wouldn't believe that her fondest wish had been granted if Elaine spent the evening shooting daggers at him with those lovely eyes of hers. He slowed the car and turned onto the gravel lane leading to his sister's lakeside home.

"Annette is my first concern. Taking that into consideration, let's not ruin dinner by squabbling in front of her, okay?"

"That's a medical bag in back, not a soapbox," Elaine said, returning his heart-stopping smile with one that she knew was less than perfect. He's a walking advertisement for his business, she mused, the tip of her tongue flicking over her crooked front tooth.

Her parents had wanted her to wear braces to correct the problem, which was barely noticeable. She'd stubbornly refused. What teenage girl wanted to be called Amtrak by her classmates? Her parents would have been far more successful if her orthodontist had had Stuart's straight white teeth.

Stuart had driven the lane so often that he could keep one eye on Elaine without risking an accident. Seeing her self-conscious expression, he said, "Your smile is breathtaking—it lights up your entire face."

"Thanks." She felt her face tingle and grow hot.

Stuart smiled. "I like the blush, too."

Elaine put both hands to her cheeks. Good grief, she thought, nurses don't blush. Thoroughly familiar with the human body and its functions, she realized that Stuart Cimarron was having a curious effect on the part of her mind that regulated her heart rate, her breathing. As a nurse, she knew these were warning signals of imminent danger, signals that shouldn't be ignored.

Dangerous? she mused, studying his profile. She felt perfectly safe. Until this moment, the only men she'd ever considered dangerous had been patients who'd been brought to the hospital where she'd worked with gunshot wounds. Unlike Stuart, they had been tough, streetwise smart alecks or hardened criminals. Their compliments hadn't made her blush. Stuart was dangerous, but not in the same sense.

"Shall we?" Stuart asked, beginning to feel ill at ease under her intent stare. He wanted to know exactly what she was thinking. Her mobile expressions were a barometer of her thoughts.

Elaine had been so intent on figuring out why her alarm system was on alert that she hadn't realized the car's engine was no longer running. They'd arrived. Caught staring at him, she stammered, "Oh, uh..." She hadn't the vaguest idea as to what he'd asked.

"Shall we?" he repeated, amused by her puzzled expression.

Deciding his question had to be fairly innocuous, she replied, "Yes."

For half a second, Stuart seriously considered leaning forward and kissing those delectable lips of hers, but decided against it. When he kissed her, he wanted her undivided attention both before and after the kiss.

Just as he opened the car door, Annette came bounding down the veranda steps. "Watch it," he called to his sister. Then, turning, he muttered to Elaine, "Keep her from running everywhere she goes, would you? She won't listen to me."

"Don't listen to the old fussbudget," Annette said, giving her brother an affectionate hug, surprised and obviously delighted that they'd arrived together. "He thinks pregnancy is an illness."

"A little less demonstrative affection on your part would be greatly appreciated." Stuart removed a handkerchief from his back pocket and erased the smear of bright red lipstick. He glanced at it, grinned, and added for Elaine's benefit, "Note the shade of lipstick Annette wears. It will save me from making explanations later."

Annette tugged at the end of his loosened tie. "Brother dear, why would you have to explain lipstick on your collar to my midwife?"

"Wouldn't you like to know?" he teased, giving Elaine a look that could have scorched asbestos.

Mouth rounding in surprise, Annette glanced from Stuart to Elaine. She slid the tie's knot upward. "You aren't holding out on me, are you?"

Elaine didn't want to give Stuart a chance to make another remark. "Hi Annette. I love your house. What a beautiful view of the lake you have. Where's Johnny?"

Casting her brother a bewildered look, Annette nodded to the workshop a hundred yards from the house and replied, "His creative juices started flowing early this afternoon. When the master craftsman is at work, his humble wife stays out of his hair."

Annette heard a snort of laughter as Stuart opened the car door for Elaine. Surprisingly, it came from the shadowed recesses of the porch.

"Humble wife? Since when?" Johnny quizzed.

"I've always been humble—well, maybe a teeny bit humble." Pride shone in her eyes as Johnny finished wiping his hands on a towel and tossed it over his shoulder.

Johnny walked down the steps lazily, closing the distance between him and his wife.

Elaine felt Stuart's arm loop over her shoulder. His fingers toyed with a stray lock of her hair. She lifted her head and raised an eyebrow. In response, he squeezed her shoulder and gazed down at her with infinite tenderness. Only the devilry in his eyes, which Annette couldn't see, gave away his ploy.

She'd been wrong when she'd tried to guess what strategy he'd use to stop his sister from shooting arrows tipped with a home-brewed love potion. Fighting would have been easier to deal with, she thought, rolling her eyes heavenward.

"Come on," Johnny said, taking his wife's hand. "My mouth has been watering for the last half hour. Not only does my *humble* wife bake indescribably delicious pies, she fixes the best barbecued ribs in the South."

Despite their good-natured bickering, Elaine felt as though she could almost reach out and touch the love flowing between Johnny and Annette. Her blue-green eyes misted with wistfulness and a shimmer of tears. Her fingers clenched. She'd done her best to hold on to Joe's love, but it had slipped through her fingers.

Stuart brought the back of her hand to his lips, brushing his lips softly against it when he saw the flash of inner pain that brought tears to Elaine's eyes. Their eyes met. Elaine saw that the devilish spark had vanished, replaced by concern for her.

By way of explanation, she murmured, "Love like theirs is so beautiful."

"Yes." His thumb stroked the soft pad of flesh beneath her thumb. "It makes me wonder if I'm missing something, too."

"Come on, you slowpokes," Annette called over her shoulder. Her eyes widened when she viewed the intimate exchange taking place between her brother and Elaine. She nudged Johnny in the ribs and winked up at him. "We're eating dinner on the front deck. I've been baking in the kitchen. It's like an oven in there."

Elaine strode up the short flight of steps with Stuart at her heels. "Can I help bring the food out?" she offered, surveying the redwood picnic table, which was covered with a sunny yellow-and-white checked tablecloth, four place settings, condiments and a glazed pottery bowl filled with wild flowers.

"Thanks." Annette accepted the offer, anxious to get Elaine alone to find out what was going on. "Johnny, why don't you pour all of us a glass of wine?"

Following Annette into the kitchen, Elaine knew Annette was bursting with curiosity. Reluctant to get involved in Stuart's little game, she decided to answer his sister's prying questions as briefly as possible.

"Your house is lovely." Elaine surveyed the collection of Johnny's work that decorated the large oak hutch at the far end of the kitchen-dinette area. "Smells heavenly, too."

"Thanks. It's small, but perfect for the two of us." Annette patted her rounded stomach. "Johnny is building another room in the back of the house. If you find sawdust in your food, that's where it came from. By the time we have four or five kids, I figure we'll need a map to get from one add-on to the next, but I'll love it." She went to the refrigerator and removed several covered bowls. She lowered her voice to a hushed whisper to keep the men from hearing what she said. "Everything is ready. I just wanted to get you alone for a minute to find out what's going on."

"Going on?"

"Between you and Stuart," Annette said succinctly.

"Nothing much," Elaine replied, reaching for a bowl. She yanked her hand back when Annette swatted at it.

"Don't you dare grab a bowl and rush out of here. Can't you see that I'm dying of curiosity?"

"You look like a picture of health. Pregnancy suits you." Elaine picked up a carrot from a tray of fresh vegetables. Dunking it into the herb dip in the tray's center, she nibbled on the tip of the vegetable. "Delicious. Can I have the recipe?"

"Sour cream and dill. You aren't going to deny being aware of those tender little glances you're getting from Stuart, are you?"

"No. Your brother is very polite and courteous."

"Polite?" Annette gasped. "Courteous? That's not what I'm seeing. He's practically drooling!"

"You think so?" Elaine popped the remainder of the carrot into her mouth and chewed thoughtfully. "This dip is really terrific."

Annette groaned in frustration. "You think I'm prying, don't you?"

"Frankly, yes," Elaine replied.

"And you aren't going to tell me anything, are you?"

Elaine grinned angelically. "Nope. Nothing to tell. Stuart stopped by the clinic to thank me for sending him a patient. You'd asked us both for dinner, so we rode out here together."

"Terrific," Annette muttered sarcastically. "Every available female in North Carolina chases after him like he's a reincarnation of the gingerbread boy—most of them willing to blab *everything* to get on my good side—and who snags him? The one woman who seems to have lockjaw!"

Elaine lifted the tray of vegetables and started toward the sliding door that led to the deck. "Believe me, I'm not keeping secrets. There simply isn't anything to tell."

From Annette's facial expression, Elaine knew Stuart's sister thought she was prevaricating. He'd been right when he'd told her that Annette heard what she wanted to hear and believed what she wanted to believe. Bringing out a stack of Bibles and swearing there was no grand passion afoot would not convince Annette she might be wrong.

"Guess I'll just have to help things along then, won't I?" Annette said, flashing Elaine a mischievous grin. "It's time big brother found himself a wife, don't you agree?"

Elaine shifted the tray to one side and glanced at her watch. "It's six o'clock—time for dinner."

Stuart, who'd been sitting on a chaise longue, quickly jumped to his feet and slid back the door for Elaine. "How's it going?" he whispered.

"Fine. I played Wonder Woman and deflected Annette's arrows." In a louder voice, she added, "The dip is delicious. Try it."

"Does Annette need any help?" Johnny asked, removing the tray from Elaine's hands and placing it on the table.

"Everything is ready. We could use a little help carrying it out here," Elaine replied, anxious not to be cornered alone in the kitchen again.

Minutes later, they were all seated around the table. Annette and Johnny shared one bench, and Stuart and Elaine sat on the opposite side of the table. As Stuart passed the food, he didn't miss an opportunity to brush his arm against Elaine's. Without asking, he buttered two rolls and put one on her plate.

You're overdoing it, she thought, wishing she could mentally send the message in his direction. His sappy expression was becoming comical. Flirting with her was one thing, but treating her as though she were the queen of the Nile was another.

When they all had their plates heaped with ribs, potato salad, coleslaw and beans, Elaine eyed her knife and fork skeptically. Ribs coated with a liberal amount of spicy tomato sauce were among her favorite foods, but eating them without looking as though she'd gotten more on the outside than the inside was going to be difficult.

"Dig in," Annette said, picking up a rib with her fingers. "Don't worry about being messy. That's one advantage of living near the lake. After dinner we can go for a swim. I have an extra suit you can wear, Elaine.''

"I guess that's one advantage I hadn't thought of," Stuart agreed, letting his eyes roam over Elaine as though he were picturing her in a scanty bikini.

Elaine sank her teeth into the succulent meat and glanced at the smiling Annette. Couldn't Annette see through Stuart's lavish display of affection? A spurt of barbecue sauce splashed her cheek. Before she could put the rib down and bring her napkin to her face, Stuart had wiped it off.

Groaning inwardly at the spectacle he was making of both of them, she shot him a quelling look.

"Good thing I didn't barbecue steaks," Johnny said when he saw Elaine's reaction to his brother-in-law's ministrations. He chuckled aloud. "Stuart would have cut it up in itsy-bitsy pieces and fed them to you." His mischievous eyes turned toward his wife. "Ouch! Why'd you kick me?"

"I remember a time when you peeled an orange and fed slices of it to me," Annette replied, obviously charmed by the thought of Stuart hand-feeding Elaine.

"Yeah, I remember, too. Do you think our company would be interested in a demonstration of my technique for removing droplets of orange juice?" Johnny asked, staring hungrily at Annette's lips in a way that left nothing to the imagination. "Let's see. You're four months pregnant...about five months ago, we went on a picnic. Ouch! Stop kicking my shins."

"You're incorrigible," Annette complained.

"Yep," Johnny agreed readily, forking a mouthful of potato salad into his mouth. He swallowed, then looked at Stuart. "Speaking of making babies, have you changed your mind about Elaine delivering the baby here?"

Familiar with his brother-in-law's tactic of getting out of the frying pan by putting someone on the griddle, Stuart replied, "I promised Elaine we wouldn't discuss business tonight. I can't let her slave away at the clinic all day and then expect her to listen to us squabble all evening."

Annette nudged her husband and leaned toward Elaine. "My brother has already reserved a room at the hospital in Roanoke Rapids for his future children. Two, mind you, a boy and a girl, three years apart...isn't that right, brother *dear*?"

"You're exaggerating, *sweet* sister," Stuart countered. He turned toward Elaine. "Elaine and I haven't discussed children, yet."

Elaine nearly strangled on the bit of coleslaw she'd been chewing when she saw three pairs of eyes trained on her. None of them knew what a touchy subject they'd stumbled upon. Even though they'd been bantering back and forth, this wasn't the time for flippancy. She couldn't tell them: *Hey, don't worry about how many or which sex. I deliver babies. I don't make them.*

Stuart tried to save her by saying, "I'm certain, considering Elaine's work, that she'll want a big family. I don't mind. What's your favorite sport, sweetheart? Basketball or football?"

"Fishing," Elaine answered dryly. "It's something you can do alone."

Johnny leaned across the table and put one finger on Stuart's bare arm. "Sss. I think you've just been burned," he teased. Turning to his wife, he added, "Looks like your brother may turn out to be a persnickety old bachelor after all."

Elaine felt like crawling under the table to avoid looking at Stuart at that moment, but his finger curled under her chin, raising it until their eyes met.

"You wouldn't condemn me to such a fate, would you?" Stuart asked.

He's faking, Elaine reminded herself. She tried to ignore the small frown puckering his brow, the way he seemed to be holding his breath as he waited for her reply. Her throat seemed to close, preventing swallowing or speaking.

Her answer came through barely parted lips. "No."

Annette squealed and clapped her hands. "I'm willing to testify in court that I witnessed him propose to you, Elaine."

"Wait!" Elaine broke eye contact with Stuart. She disliked the idea of Stuart pretending to be madly in love with her. She wasn't going to continue to let Stuart include her in the charade. "He's kidding."

"Am I?" Stuart asked, shaking his head.

Elaine's beeper chose that inopportune moment to sound. She reflexively pressed the button to turn it off, then glanced at the telephone number displayed on top. Instantly she recognized Margery's number.

Setting Annette straight regarding Stuart's affectionate behavior would have to wait. "Excuse me, please."

"The phone's on the wall by the refrigerator," Annette called as Elaine dashed across the deck. "Better get used to it, Stuart. Midwives make house calls."

Elaine dialed Margery's number, wondering what new ailment she'd be adding to Margery's chart.

"Margery? You beeped?"

"I feel awful, Elaine. I think I may be going into labor or something."

"Lower back pain?"

"No. But my stomach hurts."

"Cramping?"

"Some."

"Have you eaten anything you normally don't eat?"

Margery groaned, then paused. "No."

"Is your husband at home?" Elaine realized she should have known better than to ask. When Tom wasn't on a tractor working the fields he was in a boat fishing.

"No. He's gone fishing. The girls are here. They'll keep an eye on me till you get here."

"I'll be there in fifteen or twenty minutes." Elaine heard another low groan. Should she call the doctor she kept on standby for emergencies? From what she'd heard Elaine was fairly certain Margery wasn't going into labor. "I'm on my way. Will you be okay for ten or fifteen minutes?"

"Yeah, but hurry."

Elaine hung up the phone, grabbed her purse and began rummaging through it for her keys. Then she remembered that Stuart had driven her to his sister's house. She whispered a mild expletive. Her car was at the clinic. She should have known better than to accept a ride. Maybe Johnny would let her borrow his truck. She certainly wasn't going to ask Stuart for the keys to his Mercedes.

"I'm sorry to leave in the middle of dinner," she said as she rushed through the door, "but Margery needs me immediately. Johnny, would you mind loaning me your pickup?"

"I'll take you," Stuart offered, rising from the bench. "Your bag is in my car."

"No, really, I'd hate to spoil everyone's evening." She saw Johnny remove his keys from his pocket and place them on the table. She reached for them. "I'll—"

Stuart blocked her arm. He took her hand and started toward the car. "I insist. Margery is my patient, too. Come on."

"We both can't leave," she protested stubbornly. She glanced over her shoulder, hoping Annette would urge Stuart to finish his dinner. Annette made a shooing motion with her hand. Johnny had already returned his keys to his pocket. Trailing in Stuart's footsteps, Elaine resisted by trying to tug her hand free. "Annette went to all the trouble of preparing dinner. It's bad enough that I'm leaving. I don't need to take her other guest with me," she argued as they crossed the veranda and went toward the car.

"Annette understands. It's an emergency."

"But—"

"I can't argue and drive." He opened her door. "Get in, please."

"This isn't necessary."

"Oh, but it is," Stuart said, circling the car and waving at Johnny and Annette. "How would it look if I let you ride off into the sunset without me?"

"Like your hoax backfired?"

The Mercedes surged forward when Stuart shifted into first gear. Swiftly driving down the lane, he answered, "Exactly. Wait and see. Annette will have Johnny in Roanoke Rapids being fitted for a groomsman's tuxedo tomorrow." Delighted to have his sister off his back, he winked at Elaine. "You'll have to give directions."

"Turn right. Go about five miles to the fork in the road and veer left." Elaine missed the conspiratorial gesture. Her thoughts were on her patient. "Did you administer any drugs when you worked on her teeth?"

"No. Margery surprised me. Though my intuition pegged her as someone who'd bite my fingers if I didn't freeze her entire mouth before she sat down, Margery was a champ. She took a few deep breaths, opened wide and let me fill the cavity without a wince."

"Good for Margery." Elaine pointed to the fork in the road. "Left. Go about five miles until you see a cluster of mailboxes on the left. Turn right at the next lane. She lives in the farmhouse at the crest of the hill."

She reached down between the seats for her medical bag, set it on her lap and opened it. Everything was in place. Snapping the bag shut, she silently prayed that Margery not have complications.

The car had barely stopped on the gravel drive in front of the farmhouse when Elaine sprang from the car and ran toward the children waiting on the front porch. Celeste, the older of Margery's two children, rushed down the steps.

"How's your mother?" Elaine asked as she rushed up the steps.

"Poorly. She's been groanin' and holdin' her stomach."

Elaine followed Celeste down the front hallway and up the steps into Margery's bedroom. She heard Stuart ask Sally, the younger child, to show him her favorite doll.

She looked Margery over with a practiced eye. The room was hot, which could have accounted for the perspiration beading Margery's upper lip, but Elaine wasn't going to take any chances. Her patient could have an infection that would cause a rise in temperature.

"Elaine..." Margery said, clasping her stomach. "I'm sorry I ruined your evening."

"No problem. How are you feeling?" Elaine removed a digital thermometer from her satchel.

"Sick to my stomach."

"Are you cramping?"

"I think so, but not like I did when I was in labor."

"Could you time them to see how far apart they are?" Elaine took Margery's wrist with one hand to take her pulse.

"I tried." Margery mopped her brow with the back of her hand. "They were irregular. Do you think I'm having a bad case of indigestion?"

"You ate half a watermelon after Dad left to go fishing," Margery's daughter said. She was sitting on the foot of the bed. "Or it might be that yucky liver and onions we had for dinner."

The mixture of liver, onions and watermelon is enough to make anyone sick, Elaine thought as she popped the tip of the thermometer in Margery's mouth. "Let's see if you have a temp." Turning to Celeste, she said, "Would you open the windows for your mother? There's a nice breeze coming out of the north."

Elaine turned when she heard a light tap on the door.

"Hi, Margery." Stuart greeted the other woman, but his eyes remained on Elaine. He'd been watching her treat her patient for several moments. Elaine was calm, methodical and thorough, and yet she managed to comfort her patient. He admired any nurse who could talk and take a pulse at the same time. Anxious to help, he said, "I have a roll of antacids in the glove compartment. Would that help?"

Shaking her head, Elaine replied, "Thanks for the offer, but I think baking soda and lukewarm water will provide the same relief."

Elaine preferred home remedies whenever possible. She discouraged her patients from popping pills into their mouths every time they had a twinge of discomfort. She appreciated Stuart's concern, but his interference annoyed her.

"What's he doing here?" Margery asked, attempting to sit up.

Elaine rested her hand on Margery's shoulder to keep her lying flat. Removing her stethoscope from her bag, she slid the listening device under Margery's smock and answered, "I was having dinner at Johnny and Annette's house when you beeped me. Her brother offered to drive me over here."

Stuart felt slighted by the explanation. Since he'd picked Elaine up at the clinic, she'd been . . . what was the right word? Cool? No, she'd been warm and friendly. Reserved was a better description of her behavior. It was as though something was keeping her from being carefree and flirtatious. He wondered what the reason for her behavior could be. Mystery, thy name is Elaine? he mused.

"That's a relief. One trip to the dentist a day is enough for anyone," Margery grumbled.

Elaine heard gurgling noises coming through the stethoscope. "Sounds like the watermelon is attacking the onions," she quipped, removing the instrument and returning it to her bag. Celeste had opened the window, and cooler air was beginning to circulate in the room. "Do you have an electric fan?"

"There's one in each of our rooms and one in the living room," Celeste volunteered. "Mom doesn't have one in here because Dad doesn't want anything blowing on him while he's sleeping."

"Would you mind getting one? I'd like to talk to your mother alone for a minute." Elaine could tell from the pinched expression on the child's face that she wanted to help her mother but didn't want to cross her dad. "Your mother can turn it off tonight before your dad goes to bed."

"I guess that'll be all right," Celeste said dubiously. "Mom's going to be okay, isn't she?"

"Your mother will be fine." Elaine looked at Stuart and nodded toward the doorway. He opened his mouth as though he were going to say something, then clamped it shut. "You can fix Margery a glass of water with a teaspoon of baking soda, if you would, please."

After Stuart and the child left the room, Elaine sat down on the edge of the mattress. Margery avoided looking at her by gazing at the gently swaying curtains.

"Margery, you know I'm concerned about your feeling nauseated," she said softly.

"Yeah, I know. I'm sorry I dragged you away from Annette's house."

"That's immaterial," Elaine said, dismissing the apology with a wave of her hand. "I think what is important is the reason behind your eating binge. I can treat indigestion, but I think we need to get to the root of the problem, don't you?"

Margery rolled onto her side to face the window. Her eyes closed. She folded her arms and slowly drew her knees up to her chest.

Margery was silent, but her body language almost shrieked: *Don't ask. I won't discuss it.*

Elaine scooted toward the brass headboard, bent over Margery and began massaging the taut muscles running along her spinal column and shoulders. She felt certain there was a link between Margery's eating problem and the fact that her husband spent more time on the lake than he did with his family.

Should she pry information out of Margery? she wondered. Problems that were kept bottled up had a bad habit of exploding unexpectedly. Talking usually helped.

"Margery, I want to help. Stress isn't good for you or the baby," she said calmly. She felt Margery's shoulders stiffen beneath her hands. "Whatever you say I'll keep in strict confidence."

"I'm not the kind of woman who's disloyal to the man who's putting a roof over me and my kids' heads." Her palm moved over her mouth as though having her hand clamped over her lips were the only way she could keep herself from confiding in Elaine.

"Okay, Margery," Elaine said soothingly. "I'm always available if you need me." She hoped that with each stroke of her hands she was making the bond of trust between them stronger, and that that eventually would allow Margery to speak openly. "Just call. I'll be here."

Margery reached over her shoulder and placed her hand over Elaine's. "Thanks."

For several minutes Elaine let Margery hold one hand while she continued to massage her shoulders with the other. She could feel Margery relaxing. "Go ahead and sleep. You'll feel better when you wake up."

Margery's grip on Elaine's fingers slackened until her hand fell limp on the coverlet. Careful not to jar the bed, Elaine stood. She heard the stairs creak. She moved to the door on tiptoe so as not to awaken Elaine.

"How is she?" Stuart asked softly standing at the doorway. In one hand he held a glass of cloudy water; in the other he held a fan.

"Sleeping," Elaine whispered. "She may not need the water when she wakes up, but I'll put it on the nightstand."

"The room is cooler. Do you think she'll need the fan?"

Elaine took it from him but shook her head. "I'll put it on the chest of drawers. I think she's comfortable for now."

Stuart watched Elaine gracefully cross the room. She made less noise than the rustle of material hanging over the windows. His heart seemed to swell, filling his chest until he felt as though it might burst. There was something overwhelmingly beautiful about Elaine.

She cares, Stuart mused, leaning against the doorframe as he waited. Regardless of how inconvenient it was for her to drop everything and be with her patient, Elaine cared enough not to begrudge an interruption of her personal life. Elaine's first concern was for her patients' welfare.

His esteem for her climbed another notch.

"Do you mind if we keep an eye on the kids for a while?" Elaine asked quietly once they were outside the room and going down the stairs.

The admiration she saw in his eyes was too blatant to miss. Her heart skipped a beat. She realized that, for some unfathomable reason that had nothing to do with her being his sister's midwife, his opinion of her was absurdly significant. It shouldn't be, she silently told herself, fighting the urge to lean her head against his shoulder.

"Of course not. The girls are playing tea party in the front yard." She frowned and it made him want to pull her into his arms and erase the worry lines wrinkling her brows. "There's a swing at the end of the porch. Why don't we keep an eye on them from there?"

A small smile tugged at the corners of Elaine's mouth. "I love porch swings. All of these old farmhouses have them."

"Would you trade air-conditioning for a porch swing?" Stuart asked.

"No," she replied, grinning at Margery's daughters, who were seated under a wide-branched tree, busily serving tea to their dolls. "Throw in a hammock stretched between two oaks and I'd consider buying this place."

"I know what would cinch the swap."

"What's that?"

He gestured toward the girls. "Two little darlings with dark hair and blue-green eyes playing nurse."

Elaine felt the blood drain from her face. It was as though he'd looked into the part of her mind labeled Heart's Wishes and read aloud what he'd seen there. Was her longing to have children so obvious? She'd thought she'd learned to conceal it.

"Did I say something wrong?"

"No, of course not," she said hastily, steadying the swing with one hand as she sat down.

Stuart shook his head, refusing to believe her glib denial. "Your face turned white, like someone in severe pain. Come to think of it, when I was kidding around at Annette's and asked you if you wanted a basketball team or a football team, you dodged the question."

"I answered truthfully. I do like fishing." Flustered by his direct gaze, she smoothed the front crease of her slacks. He was pacing the length of the porch as he tried to put the pieces of the puzzle together. She knew he'd find the answer within minutes if she didn't distract him. "Why don't you sit beside me? You've been on your feet most of the day, haven't you?"

Her attempt to get him talking about himself, something most men found irresistible, failed miserably. He continued pacing from the steps to the swing and back again. He stopped abruptly.

"Have you been married?"

"Yes." She reminded herself of the vow she'd made but had never had the occasion to keep. *Tell him,* her conscience urged. *Being barren isn't something to be ashamed of.* "No children."

"Your ex-husband's decision?"

He sat on the porch rail, letting one leg swing. In the split second it took Elaine to shake her head, he wondered why he was interrogating her as though she had something to hide. Millions of women were divorced and had no children. Why did it seem so odd to him that Elaine had been married but didn't have at least one child? Maybe her marriage had been brief, a total disaster.

His dark eyes followed her fingers' nervous path along the crease of her slacks. Only her hands overtly expressed her inner tension. The color had returned to her cheeks. Leave it, he silently warned himself. She isn't obligated to tell you anything.

The knot of anxiety slowly forming in the pit of his stomach told him that he had to pursue the matter now. If he backed off, she'd avoid him in the future. That thought made his stomach roll. He knew he couldn't let that happen, whatever the cost.

"How long were you married?"

"Six years."

"And you don't have children?"

Elaine heard the incredulous note in his voice. Cross him off your list of interesting males, she thought. According to his sister, he wants a family. Resigned to the fact that he'd ferret out the truth sooner or later, she said, "No, but it wasn't my choice, either."

She got up and stood next to him at the rail. She knew he was baffled. Usually, when a man and woman who were married wanted a child, they usually had one before six years had passed. Her case was the exception.

"I'd have bet money on that," Stuart muttered. "Was there an infertility problem?"

"Yes."

"His?"

Elaine took a deep breath. "Mine."

Chapter Four

Elaine scrutinized his reaction to the bomb she'd dropped. Compassion and tenderness were what she saw in the dark centers of his eyes. No pity, regret or disappointment were evident.

"And this problem caused marital stress," Stuart concluded thoughtfully. He raked his fingers over his chin as he considered what implications this information might have for their relationship.

Elaine rested her hands on the railing. Her arms stiffened as she leaned forward to ease the pain in her chest. Inhaling slowly, she replied, "Absolutely. I promised myself not to get involved with anyone who had his heart set on having a family."

"From what you've heard, I fall into that category, don't I?"

The rueful twist of his mouth increased the pressure in her chest. Breathing deeply again, she nodded. "Yes."

Stuart placed his hands on her upper arms and turned her to face him. "That's unfair. What you've heard has either come from my sister or has been a flippant response to some barb Annette made."

"Can you honestly say that you don't want children? That when you've pictured your future there haven't been kids playing a major role in the scenario?"

"I hadn't been confronted with the problem," he responded solemnly. "In all honesty, I haven't given thought to the idea of being childless. It does explain why being near you is similar to being in a hot shower when the water heater goes on the fritz and I'm pelted with icy water. You do run hot and cold."

"Purely a defense mechanism. I can't deny being attracted to you, nor can I deny trying to freeze you out." Her eyelids fluttered closed as she made the admission. "Only a masochist is eager to be hurt the same way twice."

Stuart grasped her arms tightly. He hated the thought of being responsible, even indirectly, for hurting her. She'd told him the whole truth, even though it had hurt her deeply. The shadows her eyelashes made on her cheeks emphasized her vulnerability. Her arms remained rigid beneath his hands, as though she expected him to reject her.

His lips brushed against her cheek. "I have to be as honest with you as you have been with me. Standing this close to you, smelling your fragrance, touching you, I'm incapable of rational thought. You're an exquisitely rare, beautiful woman. Intelligent. Caring. Lovable. In my wildest dreams I couldn't imagine any man who was lucky enough to be the recipient of your love being so stupid as to walk out on you."

Elaine opened her eyes to find herself mirrored in his. A whisper of heat remained where he'd lightly kissed her. She knew that if she slanted her head a fraction of an inch he'd kiss her again. A second thought hit her in the pit of her stomach: she wanted him to kiss her.

Neither of us is being rational, she thought. Deep down she knew she'd be begging for trouble if she invited his kiss.

Neither of them was a kid, easily satisfied by hand-holding and passionate kisses. They were adults—experienced adults. Even though during the last year of her marriage sex had been a living nightmare, Elaine remembered the early years, when it had been wonderful.

Neither Stuart nor I are capable of a one-night stand or a brief affair, she thought, turning away from him.

"Elaine...?"

"Stuart, this won't work for us." Her voice was barely audible as she disengaged his hands from her arms. "You haven't thought this through. Don't you understand? I can't knowingly set myself up for failure."

Frustrated, but with the gut feeling that she was right, he plowed his fingers through his dark hair and then rammed them into his pockets.

"Yeah, I do understand." His index finger tapped his temple as he added dryly, "My libido is screaming that I'm being a damned fool, but my brain will ignore it on one condition."

"Which is?"

"You won't get scared and refuse to be with me."

"I'm not afraid of you," she replied, stepping back. Her retreat spoke louder than her words, and she knew it.

You should be afraid, Stuart mused, very afraid. He was drawn to her, even though he knew he'd have to take two steps forward for every step she took backward.

A blood-curdling scream of outrage from Margery's younger daughter sent Elaine sprinting off the porch. Sally had her doll by the legs and was swinging it at her sister. "I hate you! You said you'd share, you pig!" she squealed.

"Did not!"

"Did, too!"

Celeste deflected her sister's blows with her forearm. "I'm gonna tell Mom on you for calling me a pig 'n' hittin' me."

"You started it!"

"Hey!" Elaine grabbed Sally's flailing arms and snatched the doll away from her. "Is this any way to treat your dolly?"

Tears of frustration rolled down the three-year-old's face. Grabbing her doll back, she hugged it fiercely. "I'm sorry, Maggie. I love you." She glared at her sister. "You aren't like my mean ol' sister."

"I'm gonna tell on you," Celeste exclaimed. "Mom's gonna spank you real hard."

"Shhh." Stuart's fingers were lightning-fast as they moved from his lips to circle Celeste's wrist. "Your mother is sleeping. Let's settle this between us, hmmm?"

Celeste thrust her lower lip out in a pout. "You're gonna take Sally's side 'cause she's the smallest. I get blamed for everything."

Stuart artfully dodged that trap by hunkering down, lifting Celeste up on his knee and giving her a hug. When he was younger, he'd used the same ploy to combat a grown-up from automatically siding with Annette. "What started this ruckus?"

"Celeste ate more than her share of the cookies!" Sally shouted, wiping a huge tear from her pudgy cheek.

"Did not! My doll ate one of yours."

"You fed it to her!"

"Whoa!" Elaine said. "Celeste, did you eat more than your share?"

"Yeah, but—" Celeste wrapped her arms around Stuart's neck and shot him an imploring look. "I'm bigger than Sally. I should get more cookies than her."

Celeste's childish logic had Elaine smiling inwardly, but she kept a straight face. Never having had to settle sisterly squabbles, she was at a loss as to how to settle the dispute fairly.

Stuart saved the day by saying, "Elaine, why don't you take Sally into the house. Celeste and I will clean up and be right with you."

"Sally has to help clean up!" Celeste protested loudly. "Mom says—"

Shaking his head, Stuart disengaged Celeste's arms from around his neck and set her on her feet. "You took an extra cookie because you're a big girl. Now you're going to have to earn it by cleaning up after your little sister."

"That's fair," Elaine agreed. Sally clapped her hands together and hopped from one foot to another, completely satisfied with Stuart's brand of fair play.

"I always have to do everything around here," Celeste grumbled. Reluctantly she began removing the dishes from the cloth spread on the ground.

As Elaine walked toward the porch with Sally she couldn't hear what Stuart was saying, but Celeste giggled, assuring Elaine that the minor blowup had been settled amicably.

"Can I pick a flower and take it up to Mom?" Sally asked. She pointed a short, chubby finger at a double row of marigolds and geraniums planted along the side of the house. "Mom says flowers make her feel better."

"Sure." Elaine watched as Sally scampered to the flower bed. Before she could open her mouth, the three-year-old had pinched a canary-yellow bloom from a stem. No stem, no leaves...just the blossom lay in Sally's palm as she skipped up the steps.

Elaine grinned, remembering a time when she'd been Sally's age. Her mother had asked her to fix some freshly picked green onions. Feeling very grown-up, she'd cut off the dirty white parts and arranged the dark green stems in a bowl. Like Sally, she'd only been interested in the pretty part of the plant.

Sally was halfway up the stairs by the time Elaine had the screen door open. "Sally, let's put the flower in a teacup filled with water so it will stay fresh longer."

"Mmm-kay." Sally descended the steps, jumping down the last two steps in one mighty leap as she flapped her arms. She landed on her feet. Her sundress flipped up, showing off her frilly white underpants. Proud of her feat, she straightened, grinned and asked, "Can you fly that high?"

Elaine shook her head. "No. But I know a story about a boy named Peter Pan who could fly."

Minutes later, while Stuart and Celeste were putting the tea-party dishes and tablecloth in a storage cabinet on the back porch, he heard Elaine speaking softly in the kitchen. Celeste's hearing must have been keener than his. She handed him the pile she'd carried in from the yard, put her fingers to her lips and silently entered the room. Stuart finished storing the toys, then moved to the doorway.

What he saw when he walked into the living room made a lump form in his throat. Elaine was sitting in a rocking chair. The two girls were cuddled against her chest, one on each knee. The rapt expression on the youngsters' faces, and the tenderness Elaine showed them, enchanted Stuart. Mentally he snapped a picture of the cozy scene.

She'd make a wonderful mother, he thought. Remembering the discussion they'd had earlier, knowing she'd never have children of her own, made his heart ache. Hundreds of women had unwanted babies every day. And here was a woman who'd give anything to have a child but was unable to conceive. Life could be so damned unfair.

Sighing inwardly, Stuart turned and slowly climbed the steps. Elaine had the children under control; he'd make himself useful by checking on their mother.

Margery sat up in bed, yawning and stretching. Naps were a rarity, a luxury she could seldom indulge in with two active children. She heard heavy footsteps coming up the stairs. She glanced outside at the fading sunlight, then at her wristwatch.

Panicking, she swung her legs off the bed. Any thought of her earlier discomfort was forgotten. Huffing and puffing, she muttered, "What's he doing home before midnight? He'll skin me alive if he catches me laying in bed with company taking care of the girls."

"Margery?" Stuart heard the movement in the bedroom. "Are you okay?"

Relieved to know it was Dr. Cimarron rather than her husband climbing the steps, Margery crossed the room and called, "I'm fine. How are the girls doing?"

"Elaine is telling them a story." He gave her a quick once-over. The fine lines of fatigue that had been etched around her eyes had nearly disappeared. She no longer laced her fingers beneath her protruding stomach as though she were carrying a too-heavy burden. "No aches or pains?"

"Fresh as a daisy," Margery replied, scooting through the doorway. "The girls haven't given you any trouble, have they?"

"They're good kids," Stuart replied evasively. Far be it from him to snitch on them for quarreling. "Sally looks as though she's about to fall asleep on Elaine's lap."

"It's early to bed, early to rise around here. I appreciate the two of you giving me a breather."

Margery went down the steps with Stuart following her.

"Mommy!" Celeste squealed. She jumped down from Elaine's lap, ran across the hardwood floor and put her arms around her mother's knees. "Do you know the peanut butter story?"

"Peter Pan?" Margery asked, making the connection between the commercial and the children's story. She mussed Celeste's hair affectionately and squeezed her slender shoulders.

"Uh-huh," Celeste said. "I like Tinkerbell the best. She flies around helping Peter. She saved him from a crocodile and everything. I'm gonna be just like her from now on."

Elaine looked down at Sally, who was asleep in her arms. Gently, so as not to awaken her, she combed a damp lock of hair off her forehead. I wish I had a precious little girl like you, she thought to herself. With an almost imperceptible shake of her head, she brought herself out of the children's world of pixie dust and impossible dreams.

Lifting Sally in her arms, Elaine stood. "Sally picked a flower for you. She fell asleep before she could give it to you. Mind if I tuck her in?"

"I'll carry her upstairs," Stuart said, holding out his arms. Recalling Celeste's distress over Sally getting special treatment, he added, "How about letting me tuck you in, Celeste."

"Neato," Celeste exclaimed, unwinding her arms from her mother's legs. She rushed toward the steps. "Last one in bed is a rotten turnip."

Elaine surrendered Sally to Stuart's strong arms. Quite by accident, the back of his forearm grazed against her breast as the child was transferred. Against her will, her nipples reflexively tightened, straining against the front of her cotton shirt. Sensual awareness flooded through her. She hadn't had a man touch her since her husband.

As she followed him upstairs, her mind took a flight into fantasy. Under other circumstances, this situation might have been real. She might have been following her husband upstairs looking forward to the nightly routine of putting their children to bed.

Under other circumstances, she reminded herself. Her situation wasn't likely to change. Stuart wasn't her husband. Celeste and Sally weren't her children. The physical hunger she'd felt when he'd touched her wouldn't be satisfied after the children were asleep. No, she thought, she'd have to be content with the few precious moments she'd been given.

"Sally's bedroom is next to mine," Celeste said in a hushed tone, ducking into her room to hastily change into her pajamas. "Her nightie is under the pillow."

Elaine stepped around Stuart to turn the bed-clothes down, then immediately moved to the dresser. She'd heard Celeste tell Stuart the nightie was under the pillow, but she wasn't going to take a chance on being too close to Stuart. She had to fight her fantasy, and the reality of his physical appeal.

Careful not to awaken Sally, Stuart laid her on the bed. "I haven't had much practice undressing little girls," he whispered, admitting his inadequacy without feeling self-conscious.

"Only big girls?" Elaine said dryly, moving to the bed after Stuart had taken several steps back. As she reached under the pillow to find Sally's nightgown, she felt a playful slap on her backside.

"Big girls know how to get undressed all by themselves," was his ready reply. "They don't need my help."

He was out of the room before Elaine could think of a comeback. "He probably specializes in cosmetic dentistry," she muttered too late.

Sally was as limp as a Raggedy Ann doll, Elaine silently observed as she tried to remove the little girl's sundress and pull her nightie over her head. Elaine snuggled the bedclothes under her little pointed chin. Then, unable to resist, she hummed a few strains of the lullaby her mother had sung to her when she'd been a child.

She was still humming when she left the bedroom and went downstairs. In the living room, Margery sat in front of the television set watching a game show and eating popcorn.

"Thanks for putting the kids to bed. Want some popcorn?" Margery asked, passing the bowl.

"Buttered?"

"No."

"Salted?" Elaine took a few kernels and popped them into her mouth for a taste test.

"Just a little bit. You said fresh fruit and popcorn were nature's snack foods. Salt comes from the earth, too, even if it does make people retain water."

"This is perfect," Elaine commented, complimenting Margery. "Remember what the Greeks said: everything in moderation. None of the foods you ate today were harmful—only the amount."

Margery grinned, examining a kernel of popcorn thoughtfully. "I watch what I eat. If it doesn't stare back at me, I figure I'm safe."

"Um-hmmm. You aren't safe when the watermelon, onions and liver are waging all-out war. Throw in a couple of popcorn hand grenades and you'll be upstairs moaning and groaning again."

"I'm a slow learner sometimes, but pain leaves a lasting impression." She deposited the popcorn bowl on the coffee table and gave it a shove. Pointing her finger at her chest, she said, "I know what causes these food binges. I'm the only person who can stop them."

Elaine kept her mouth shut, hoping Margery trusted her enough to go into detail. Steps creaked as Stuart returned downstairs, interrupting what Margery might have revealed.

"They're both asleep," Stuart remarked, extending his hand to Elaine to help her off the sofa. When he saw Margery begin to get to her feet, he said, "Please. Don't get up. Is there anything else we can do for you before we go?"

"Nothing, but thanks for driving Elaine over here and for helping out with the girls." She winked at Elaine. "You two run along and have a good time. There should be a full moon tonight."

The world is full of cupids, Elaine thought, as she took Stuart's hand. His eyes lighted up with mischief, warning her that he wouldn't mind continuing the charade he'd played at his sister's house.

"Guess I'd better get home before the werewolves come out," Elaine joked. She eyed Stuart's chin suspiciously. "I've read that some wolves shave their whiskers off to fool unsuspecting maidens."

"The better to keep the maiden from getting a whisker burn," Stuart muttered for her ears only. He chuckled at the idea of his being called a wolf. He hadn't had to do anything to lure women into his house in the past, and he'd certainly never dressed up as a grandmother.

Joining in the fun, Margery added, "And they go to dentists to have their fangs filed down. Of course, if the wolf happens to be a dentist, I guess that isn't necessary."

"Poor, maligned wolves," Stuart said, shaking his head in mock sorrow. He tucked Elaine's hand in the crook of his arm, leaned toward her, smiled wickedly and growled, "They mate for life. The ones you hear howling at the moon are doing it because they've lost their mate."

"Is that true?" Elaine asked, intrigued by the idea of a wild animal falling in love and being faithful.

"Yes except for the howling-at-the-moon part." He patted her hand affectionately. "I've always thought

'Little Red Riding Hood' was a gruesome tale. I can think of a much better ending."

"Such as?" Elaine let him lead her toward the screened door.

"The maiden kissing the wolf, changing him into a fun-loving wolf who'd lavish hot, wet kisses on her. He'd love her forever and ever."

Margery giggled girlishly. "That sounds better than waiting for the hunter to run into the house and kill the wolf. Ugh! I know who'd have to clean up the mess."

"On that gory note," Stuart said as he ran his finger around his loosened shirt collar, "I think we'd better leave—otherwise you two ladies won't invite me back again."

"Dr. Cimarron, you're always welcome here." Margery waved in their direction.

"Night," Elaine called over her shoulder. "I'll see you next week at the clinic."

When Elaine was seated in the car, she turned to Stuart and asked thoughtfully, "Do you think a married woman with two children could be lonely?"

"I'd say it depends on the woman. Margery? Yeah, probably. You? I seriously doubt you'd be lonely." He started the engine and proceeded down the winding lane.

"What's the difference between the two of us?"

"Fishing."

"For compliments?" Elaine asked. Trees canopied the lane, making it difficult for Elaine to see if Stuart was teasing her again.

"I meant the rod-and-reel type of fishing. From the comments made by the kids, I think Margery is a prime example of a fishing widow." He picked up her hand and nibbled on her fingertips. "As for your fishing for compliments, I'm not a man who makes flowery speeches, but..."

A tiny electrical current spread from her fingers and traveled up her arm, straight to her heart. She jerked her hand away from his teasing lips and folded her hands together in her lap. She heard his low chuckle at her instinctive reaction.

"You're a horrid tease," she said accusingly.

"Yes. I admit it."

"Can't you be serious for five seconds?"

"Yes. But I'd rather enjoy a moonlight ride with a particularly attractive brunette with emerald-blue eyes brighter than the closest star."

"My eyes are blue," Elaine replied, flattered that he'd noticed the yellow flecks that often made them appear green. "You can change the endings of fairy tales. You can't change my eye color to suit your preference."

Stuart grinned. "Wanna bet?"

A break in the hovering trees allowed the moon to light the car's interior. Elaine saw a decidedly wolfish smile on his face. "Your fangs are showing," she quipped, hugging the door.

"There's a file in the glove compartment."

Elaine was about to make a snappy retort about a dentist who carried the tools of his trade along with him when she remembered that she'd forgotten her own medical bag.

"Oh, shoot. Stop the car."

Gravel crunched under the Mercedes's tires as Stuart slammed on the brakes. He'd always considered himself lucky where women were concerned, but he hadn't expected Elaine to order him to park on a lonely, deserted lane. Who was he to argue?

"Can you turn around?" Elaine queried, leaning toward him and looking over her shoulder for the nearest wide place in the road.

"It's been years since I've necked in a car, but I seem to recollect that I hunched down in the seat and the girl sort of sat on my lap," he answered dryly.

Realizing how he'd interpreted her command, Elaine burst out laughing. Claire had told her of the feminine ploys other women had used to snare North Carolina's most eligible bachelor. He'd accused Elaine of running hot and cold. Did he really believe she'd turned up the thermostat to the boiling point and couldn't wait until they were in a more circumspect place? Lord have mercy, she hadn't necked on a wilderness road when she'd been a teenager.

"I've admitted that it's been a while, but I don't seem to recollect a lot of laughter at this point." Amused by his obvious mistake, he glanced in the rearview mirror. "Nope. No spinach between my teeth. Care to tell me what's tickling your funny bone?"

"Medical bag," Elaine gasped between bursts of laughter.

"Is that the punch line of a joke?"

"No," she gasped, covering her mouth to stifle her chuckles. "I asked you to stop because I forgot my medical bag. You'll have to turn around so I can go back and get it."

"And here I thought I was going to get a chance to win my bet." Stuart shifted into reverse and turned the car around. "Your eyes appear green when you're laughing and when you're angry. Makes a man wonder whether or not passion has the same effect."

Elaine didn't know what color her eyes were when she made love, but his words stunned her. Her jaw dropped, and her mouth felt parched. She couldn't breath, much less laugh.

"Speechless? No smite-thee-down-with-the-jaw-bone-of-an-ass comeback?"

Nodding, Elaine focused her eyes on a pair of red taillights ahead of them on the gravel road.

"Lady, you're a bundle of contradictions," he murmured. "A nurse, particularly a midwife, should not be the least bit embarrassed to discuss sex. And yet you are. You, my dear midwife, are a very, very mysterious lady."

And you, my dear dentist, aren't going to be given an opportunity to solve the mystery, she thought. Any man who can come between me and my medical bag is too dangerous to be called a friend.

Minutes later, after Elaine had collected her bag and was seated beside him again and they were close to the main road, Stuart realized he actually resented having to share Elaine with the demands of her career. He could pretend he didn't mind, but that was exactly what it would be—pretending. He wanted her undivided attention. He didn't want to end the evening by chauffeuring her home from a house call. "How do you feel about going for a spin on the lake? Maybe anchor the boat and take a swim?''

Elaine hesitated before answering. On such a hot, sultry night, the thought of skimming across the lake with only moonbeams to light their way held great appeal. She loved the idea of swimming without being restricted by the wall of a pool.

Common sense warned her to go back to her apartment above the clinic. Stuart's magnetic charm was too compelling to ignore. His ability to make her laugh when she intended to keep him at arm's length by carrying on a serious discussion was too disarming.

Laughter was nature's best medicine for healing old wounds. She'd read that somewhere, probably in one of the pop psychology magazines. It didn't take an advanced degree in psychology to know she was vulnerable to the man sitting beside her, waiting patiently for her answer.

"I'm afraid to jump in water over my head when I can't see what's on the bottom," she answered.

Stuart didn't have to look at Elaine to know she was worrying her bottom lip between her teeth. Her reply smacked of evasiveness, he was sure it had a double meaning. "Don't worry about hitting your head on a stump. The cove I usually swim in is safe. You aren't going to be out in the middle of the lake swimming alone. I'll be there if you get into trouble."

Elaine slanted a look at him. "I don't think a midnight swim with you is a good idea," she said honestly.

"Maybe not," he admitted, meeting her direct reply just as directly. "But I know I'd be kicking myself later for being cowardly if I didn't ask."

"I'd be out of my mind to accept." *You'd be out of your mind to refuse,* her libido countered. *What can happen?*

"I'm in touch with that feeling." His refusal to accept the thought of taking her home, shaking her hand and driving back to Roanoke Rapids without kissing her was crazy. Insane. Utterly mad. And yet he knew he wouldn't get a wink of sleep until he'd felt his arms around her, felt her lips tremble beneath his. Obsessed with the thought, he added, "That's Annette's lane on the left. Unless you prefer skinny-dipping, I'm going to stop there and pick up a swimsuit for you."

In less than ten seconds he'd be heading toward his sister's cabin and the decision would be out of her hands. She opened her mouth, fully intending to tell him to bypass the lane and turn onto the highway that led into town. "Fine."

The lazy smile he gave her made her feel as though he'd pinned a medal on her chest for valor above and beyond the call of duty. She glanced over her shoulder when he made the turn, wondering if she was about to make the second biggest mistake of her life.

"The lights are out," Stuart observed a few minutes later. "Johnny and Annette must have already gone to bed."

Taking advantage of the temporary reprieve fate had granted her, Elaine blurted out, "We shouldn't awaken them. Annette needs her sleep."

"No problem. The extra swimsuits are on the back porch. I can be in and out of there without awakening them." He turned off the headlights and stopped the car. "See the boathouse over there? I'll grab the suits and meet you there."

Stuart didn't risk waiting for an affirmative reply. He was out of the car and heading for the back of the cabin before Elaine could change her mind.

You're asking for trouble, Elaine told herself. Why didn't you say no? A thousand times no?

Because you dread the thought of going home and sweltering in your apartment, she silently replied. She was so keyed up that she knew sleep would evade her. What the hell, you're here. Enjoy yourself for a change.

Sighing, Elaine got out of the car and followed the path toward the boathouse.

Moments later, Stuart caught up with her. He must have beaten the world record for the hundred-yard dash, she mused. "That was fast," she said.

"Yep." Too winded to give her a lengthy explanation, he handed her the two-piece suit clenched in his hand. When they reached the boathouse, he flipped a light switch. Yellow light from a naked bulb hanging over a speedboat flooded the interior. Pointing toward a closed door, he said, "You change in the storage room while I change on the boat. Watch out for Johnny's fishing tackle."

Elaine entered the small room and shut the door. Instantly enveloped in darkness, she called, "Is there a light in here?"

"Raise your hand over your head and circle it."

Automatically following his directions, Elaine reached up. A thin cord wrapped around her wrist. She pulled it downward. She unzipped her dress and examined Annette's suit at the same time. It was navy blue, with small white polka dots. She shed her shoes, dress and underclothing, staring at the bikini and wondering if Stuart had hastily grabbed a child's suit by mistake.

Hospitals have larger Band-Aids, she groaned silently. It certainly wasn't a suit to wear in broad daylight or in public. Mentally praying for clouds to block the moonlight, she slipped into the scanty garment. She hooked her thumbs beneath the fabric to stretch it over her behind. The elastic stretching over her hips inched lower, but she could still feel a good portion of rounded buttocks uncovered. She sucked her flat stomach in, pulled up the elastic band and tried again. Forget it. There was simply more of her than there was of the suit.

She had a similar problem when she hooked the front clasp on the suit's top. Although she supposed she was amply endowed, she'd never considered herself busty. The underwiring cupped her breasts, lifting them and pushing them toward the lacy edge of the top, forming a deep V of cleavage.

My underwear covers the subject better, she thought. But she knew that once they were wet, her bra and panties would become transparent.

"Does it fit?" Stuart called. Rolling his clothes into a ball, he stashed them under the front seat of the boat. Johnny had left the key dangling from the switch instead of hiding it under the passenger seat, as he usually did.

"I didn't realize how small your sister is," Elaine responded. She pulled the light cord and plunged the tackle room in darkness. She wasn't about to have the light shining behind her when she stepped from the room. If only she could reach the other light switch and plunge the entire boathouse into total darkness.

"It might not be hers," Stuart confessed. "I felt a one-piece suit hanging behind that one, but I figured a two-piece suit would fit better."

Embarrassed to the very core of her being, Elaine tried to work up the courage to step out of her hiding place. Other women wear less at public pools, she thought. You've nothing to hide. No bulges. No paunch. No weight. What's the worst that can happen? He could laugh, fall overboard and drown. She shrugged her slender shoulders.

"One little chuckle and I'll pitch him overboard myself!" she muttered. For good measure, she added, "And applaud while he thrashes around."

Suddenly the silence was broken by the speedboat's engine roaring to life, and Elaine jumped. Her arm pushed against the door, and she was standing in the opening before she recovered her wits. Assuming the poise of a fashion model walking down a runway, she strolled to the open bow of the boat.

Stuart's throat worked hard to swallow as he watched her step gracefully toward him. Her street clothes had concealed her striking, exquisitely feminine curves. His dark, smoldering eyes traveled up her

shapely legs to the slight flare of her hips, then proceeded upward to her narrow waist and full breasts.

To steady the boat while she boarded, he held on to
the dock. She grabbed the front rail, turned, pointed
her toe and stepped backward onto the seat cushion.
The suit's French-style legs revealed the cutest tush
he'd ever had the pleasure of viewing. Though it was
almost midnight, he felt as though the sun's hottest
rays were scorching his skin.

Hoping the low throbbing of the outboard engine
was louder than the sound of him clearing his throat,
he asked, "Ready?"

Chapter Five

Elaine reclined on the cushion in the bow of the boat. She could have seated herself next to Stuart, but she'd decided her skin was hot enough to ignite. Distance would provide relative safety. "I'm ready when you are."

Stuart reached for the throttle. Just in time to avoid making a total fool of himself, he remembered to untie the rope from the dock. Concentrating on getting the boat out of the slip without destroying the dock, he eased the throttle back.

He hadn't laughed at her, Elaine mused gratefully, but how was she supposed to interpret his silence? She stretched one leg forward and curled her foot under her thigh. Expecting him to swing the boat away from the cove and head toward the wide expanse of Gaston Lake with the throttle wide open, she braced one arm behind her and held the guardrail tight with the other. He surprised her by keeping the throttle just above the idle position. Slow and easy, she thought, relaxing her grip.

"Gorgeous night," Stuart said when the silence became overpowering. Gorgeous woman, he silently added.

Moonlight spread across the mirror-smooth surface of the lake like candle flames. The cabins tucked among the towering trees were nothing more than inky-black shadows. From across the lake, Elaine could hear the faint, sorrowful wailing of a saxophone playing a blues tune. Elaine closed her eyes and let the music wash over her. There was something about the melody that seemed to reach out and grab her.

"Bob York must be at his lake house," Stuart commented when he heard the music. "*Time* magazine says he's considering retiring from show business."

"Bob York owns a cabin here?" Elaine asked, astonished.

Stuart chuckled softly. "Not a cabin, exactly. His house is a bit fancier than his neighbors'."

"Have you met him?" Elaine had been a fan of the talented saxophonist since she'd been a teenager. She had a complete collection of his record albums. She especially liked an album of his on which he'd taken old standards and jazzed them up with his own fresh, unique style. Depending on what tune he played, he could make her feel like weeping, or singing, or strutting around like the sexiest woman on earth.

"Once. He came in for emergency treatment. I didn't connect the name on the information card with his face. His jaw was twice its normal size. It wasn't until later, when I received two front-row tickets to a concert at North Carolina State, that I realized I'd taken out one of Bob York's wisdom teeth."

Elaine grinned. "His tooth wouldn't exactly qualify as a conversation piece to display on your coffee table," she said lightly.

"You're right, but my receptionist was furious I never told her that my patient was *the* famous Bob York. She condensed a month's worth of dirty looks into a couple of days. I gave her the tickets to his concert to keep peace in the office."

Stuart steered the boat into an uninhabited cove and cut the engine. Moving to the rear of the boat, he released the catch that held the boat's anchor in place, then lowered the ladder over the side.

Despite what she'd said earlier about being afraid of jumping into water over her head, Elaine closed her eyes and dived off the front of the boat, barely making a splash. The lake water felt cool, silky, invigorating. She swam below the surface for several yards, then opened her eyes and watched millions of tiny air bubbles rush up toward the moonlight. Surfacing, she rolled onto her back and leisurely backstroked away from the boat.

Stuart heard the splash as she dived. Quickly he moved to the bow. He was standing on the seat cushion when she surfaced. It unnerved him when he realized how much he wanted to race after her, pull her into his arms and feel each luscious inch of her bare skin pressed against him. A surge of passion jolted through him when her eyes opened and she looked at him. Her eyes glistened, bright as a fiery diamond. Her dark hair, wet and sleek, was gilded with silver moonlight. The moonlight shone down, bright and clear, and he decided to take the plunge rather than let Elaine see the effect she had on him.

Something primitive, perhaps the desire to be the hunter instead of the hunted, made him keep his dive shallow and then swim fast until he reached her side.

Stretched flat on her back, Elaine let her muscles relax until she could keep afloat just by moving her hands. "Heavenly," she whispered. "Just... heavenly."

"My sentiments exactly," Stuart said, floating on his back and drifting close to her.

For long moments they lay beside each other. Occasionally their bodies touched as they maintained their prone positions by moving their arms and legs slightly.

"Mermaids have it made," she sighed contentedly. "Nothing to do in life but swim around and rule over the lesser fish."

"And entice callow young men into the sea's depths," he said, deliberately baiting her. Touching her casually wasn't enough. He wanted an excuse to wrap his arms around her. Any pretext would do. A water fight seemed as good as any.

"Fantasy spoiler," she cried, splashing droplets of water on his chest as she jackknifed and let her feet sink.

Ready for his retaliation, she prepared to make a hasty retreat to the boat. One downward thrust of his shoulders would give her a head start. She swam a little closer, watching his face for an indication of his intent.

What she saw in his eyes had nothing to do with getting even for being splashed. She easily discerned desire, raw hunger and need.

It wasn't fear of him that made her strike out for the boat: it was fear of her own response. Face-to-face with his desire, she realized that the empty feeling in the pit of her stomach had nothing to do with having missed dinner.

Her freestyle stroke was jerky as she propelled herself toward the boat. With each stroke, her subconscious offered excuses for the gnawing ache plaguing her. She hadn't been with a man for a long, long time. Sex-starved? she asked herself, repelled by the idea of being a woman who couldn't be around a man without picturing herself making love to him. No, no, no, she thought with every stroke. She wasn't like that. Dammit, it had been sex that had finally driven her into the divorce courts.

Lovemaking wasn't always bad, her heart told her vehemently. Only when it lost its spontaneity... only when the results became more important than the loving... only when the love in your heart shriveled and died...

Her arm struck the back of the boat. Suddenly she wondered if she'd been swimming in the wrong direction. Should she have been swimming toward Stuart instead of away from him? She wasn't immune to desire. She was still young, still a healthy woman with normal desires. Stuart wanted her. The attraction was mutual. Why should she deny giving him what they both wanted? So what if she couldn't get pregnant? She'd kept her promise to herself. She'd told him a permanent relationship was impossible because she couldn't have children. Stuart wouldn't expect anything she couldn't give him.

She held on to the chrome ladder, wiping her hair back from her face. Good grief, she silently moaned. She'd almost convinced herself that making love with Stuart would be mutually satisfying. She knew better. Other women could surrender their bodies to a near stranger without emotional commitment, but she wasn't one of them.

Sex without love—it had destroyed her marriage and had almost destroyed her. She wasn't going to let physical attraction destroy what remained of her self-esteem. The price of casual sex was too high, plain and simple.

A shout came from beyond the bow. "Elaine?"

"I'm getting in the boat," she called, grabbing both sides of the rail as she raised her foot up to the bottom step. The ladder wasn't designed for someone her height to use with ease. It took her last ounce of strength and determination to heave herself into the boat.

Stymied, Stuart slapped the lake's surface with the flat of his hand. He pumped his legs to keep afloat. "Peddling like a maniac and getting nowhere fast, barely keeping afloat!" he muttered, chagrined by the present state of affairs.

He hadn't the vaguest idea as to what he'd done to offend her. For pete's sake, all he'd done was look at her. It wasn't as though he'd undressed her and ravished her nubile body.

The sound of the boat's motor cut short his confusion. Dammit! She was going to drive off and leave him stranded in the middle of the lake!

"Elaine!" he roared. The boat eased forward toward him. He dived away from the oncoming boat, and his face was underwater when he bellowed, "Damn!" Whatever I did, it wasn't bad enough for her to want to mangle me with the propeller! he added silently. He surfaced and gulped air into his oxygen-starved lungs. He waved his arms above his head to stop her. "Are you crazy? Whattaya think you're doin'?"

"Coming to get you," she answered calmly. She pushed the throttle down another inch. The engine raced, but the distance between the boat and Stuart didn't narrow. "What's wrong with you? Why are you swimming away from the boat? Darn it, Stuart Cimarron, stop playing around and get in the boat!"

"Playing around?" he repeated. "You think I'm playing around?"

"Aren't you? Just because the rest of the female population chases after you doesn't mean I'm going to join them. So help me, if you don't get in the boat I'm going to let you swim to shore and walk back to Annette's."

Stuart shook his head as though he had water in his ears and hadn't heard her properly. Her hot-and-cold treatment must have finally pushed him to the brink of insanity. One of them was going mad, that was for damned certain.

"Turn off the engine," he shouted, not taking any chances. "Take the key from the ignition and hold it up in your hand where I can see it."

"Might as well," Elaine muttered. "It isn't running right anyway."

She pulled the throttle back, twisted the key to the off position, pulled it out and held it dangling over her head. Much to her dismay, she felt the boat move backward. What the hell was going on? she wondered.

None too patiently, she waited for Stuart to swim to the boat and climb aboard. Her plan to cruise up to him, get him aboard and get out of temptation's path had been a dismal failure. When she felt the boat shift as Stuart started up the ladder, she tossed the keys on the dash, folded her arms on the steering wheel and rested her forehead on them.

Out of breath, Stuart panted, grabbed a towel and began wiping the water from his face. "What happened out there?"

"Nothing."

"Nothing?" He flung the towel on the floor and sat down on the seat beside her. "One minute the lake is like our private water bed, and the next minute you're plowing through the water as though you'd woken up and found a rapist next to you." He took a deep breath. "You're driving me *crazy*!"

She could have told him what she'd seen in his eyes, Elaine mused, but in his present state she knew he'd deny it. The best thing to do, she decided, was to wait until he'd stopped ranting and raving and then quietly ask him to fix the boat and take her back to Annette's cabin.

"Say something," he demanded. "Explain."

"Nothing to explain."

"You're going to calmly sit there with your head buried in your arms and tell me 'nothing,' when you just tried to run over me with the boat?"

Shocked by his accusation, she replied frostily, "I'm a registered nurse. I patch people up, not cut them up."

"I heard you very clearly. You said 'I'm coming to get you.' Deny it!"

He'd quoted her accurately, she thought, but hurting him wasn't what she'd had in mind. Was this some sort of strange joke he was pulling on her? She cocked her head to one side and looked at him. The smile she was used to seeing on his lips had vanished, replaced by a thin, straight line. His square jaw thrust toward her aggressively. There wasn't a smidgen of humor dancing in his eyes.

"I would never hurt you," she replied in a flat voice.

"Lady, one way or another, you're killing me. I can't even think straight." His hands raked through his wet hair. Exasperated with himself for jumping to the wrong conclusion for the second time in one evening, he sat down in the driver's seat, put his elbows on his knees and leaned toward her. Earnestly he said, "Talk to me, Elaine. Tell me what the hell happened out there. What's going on in that beautiful head of yours?"

Elaine straightened her arms, leaned back against the seat and stared blankly at nature's lavish display of stars as she sorted through her thoughts.

She did feel as though she owed him some sort of rational explanation for her behavior. He'd been the the perfect Southern gentleman the entire evening, offering her a ride to Annette's dinner party, dropping everything when she'd received an emergency call, listening to her problems without reacting negatively, and making her laugh whether she wanted to or not. Yes, she silently admitted, he deserved better treatment from her.

Swimming away from him had been an attack of cowardice brought on by her own errant longings. How in the world was she going to be able to explain that without sounding utterly ridiculous? She worried her bottom lip between her teeth.

"Just tell me what you're thinking," he said encouragingly. "And what you're feeling."

"In the water..." she began hesitantly, "...I confused what I thought I saw in your eyes with what I was thinking." Great beginning, she told herself, knowing she wasn't making sense. Stop generalizing and be specific. "I mean...I thought you wanted to kiss me, when actually it was *me* wanting to kiss *you*."

Stuart was tempted to interrupt and admit that he'd been aching to kiss her long before they'd arrived at the lake. He kept his mouth shut.

"That's not the whole truth," she said, deciding to be totally honest. "I, uh, I was thinking about more than kissing." She glanced at him covertly to gauge his

reaction. He hadn't moved a muscle. She had his undivided attention.

"It's been a long, long time since I've thought about
making love. Considering the fact that I'm divorced
because the bedroom of my home became a battlefield, I guess my wanting you is inconsistent, huh?"

"No," Stuart answered swiftly, softly.

"It is to me."

"Why?"

"Because I've always believed love and making love
were inseparable." Her eyes met his. Her voice
dropped to a whisper. "I don't love you, and yet...
See? I told you I'm confused."

Without conscious thought, he raised his hand to
touch her face. Certain he'd be rebuffed, he stopped
it in midair. Knowing that she wanted him and at the
same time knowing that she'd fight him tooth and nail
was tearing him apart.

For a man who'd remained single while other men
his age had married and started families, the concept
of love and making love being intertwined was foreign to him. He wasn't cavalier. There weren't any
notches on his bedposts. He didn't hang out in singles
bars hoping to score. He'd genuinely cared for the
women he'd slept with. Sexuality to him was as natural as eating or sleeping.

Stuart laced his fingers together to keep from
brushing the stray wisps of dry hair back from her
face. It pleased him immensely to learn the attraction
he'd felt was mutual. But he was smart enough to realize he wanted more from her than just seduction.
Right now, she was weak and confused, uncertain of

what she wanted. He wanted her strong, willing, wanting more than a sexual playmate.

His thinking went a step farther than it had ever gone with other women.

Much to his consternation, he realized exactly what he wanted: he wanted those emerald-blue eyes of hers to be shining with love when she looked at him.

During Stuart's silence, Elaine saw his facial expression change. At first the grim brackets on each side of his mouth expressed anger. Then his facial muscles relaxed, changing his expression to one of deep contemplation. Finally his forehead smoothed and his jawline hardened. She knew he'd made a decision. She hoped they both could live with it.

"Remember Bob York's rendition of the song 'Just one of those Things'? I think Frank Sinatra made the original recording." He hummed a few bars of the melody. "The lyrics could have been written for two people like us. It was about a love affair that was too hot not to cool down. The song ended with the couple parting, saying they'd meet now and then. They'd be friends. Remember it?"

"Umm-hmmm. It's one of the few albums that has someone singing. When I first listened to it I wondered if the lyrics were a special message to someone."

Stuart lifted his head toward the sky. "I don't want to blame what we're feeling on a flight to the moon on gossamer wings, or physical chemistry, or rampant hormones. But I have a sinking sensation in my stomach that tells me unless you get to know me, unless you learn to trust me, you're going to blame what you're feeling on one of those three things. Like the lyrics to the song, you'll cool down and just want to be friends."

A wry smile curved her lips. "Swapping patients instead of kisses?"

"Now who's joking around when the other person is being serious?" he said mildly, returning her smile.

"Sorry. Levity relieves tension."

"True, but flippancy is like putting a temporary filling in a patient's mouth. It gives temporary relief, but it doesn't correct the problem." Stuart's eyes dropped from her eyes to her full bottom lip. Kissable, he mused, wondering how the hell he was going to make it through the next five seconds without kissing her.

Action, his mind shouted. Don't sit there fantasizing about how she'll taste and what response you'll get. Get up!

Stuart heard the commands and started to react, but seeing Elaine's eyes focus on his lips destroyed his good intentions. She wanted his kiss as badly as he wanted to kiss her.

A groan came from low in his chest. "Elaine, sweetheart, don't look at me like that."

"How?" Talk, like humor, hadn't relieved the sexual awareness stringing between them, drawing her toward him, tilting her head to give him free access to her lips. One kiss, she promised. Then she'd know if her mind had been playing games with her. She'd know if her worrying had been pointless. One kiss, that was all she'd need for now.

The blood pounding in his ears deafened him to her quietly spoken question. Bonds of restraint frayed, then snapped as she inched forward. He couldn't have stopped himself from responding to her inviting mouth any more than he could have walked on water to get away from her.

Sweet, incredibly sweet, she thought when his lips touched hers tentatively, brushing erotically from one corner to the other. Elaine sighed. The last remnants of tension passed through her lips. She had her answer. She'd been confused, sending him mixed signals, but her mind hadn't been playing tricks on her. His kisses were dangerous, volatile, addictive. For better or worse, she knew Stuart was the man who could change the course she'd set for herself. Falling in love with him could make her or break her—and she didn't fear the latter.

"Enough," Stuart whispered, settling his hands on her shoulders. Liar, his mind shouted. Not enough! Not nearly enough! "I'll take you home."

The regret she heard in the tone of his voice matched her own disappointment. He was being sensible. Lingering a moment longer would be imprudent. She nodded, unable to force speech through the lips he'd so thoroughly kissed. Her fingertips trembled as they touched her mouth, imprinting his kiss on her memory. It wasn't her first kiss, but it was one she'd remember for eternity.

A spray of goose bumps formed where his hands had touched her. Crossing her arms over her chest, she rubbed her hands up and down from her elbows to her shoulders.

"Cold?" Stuart asked, draping a dry towel around her shoulders.

"No. Nerves, I guess." The sound of the engine starting brought a weak smile to her lips. Something was wrong with the boat. They were stuck here. "I couldn't get the boat to go forward."

Stuart glanced over his shoulder. "Did you pull the anchor up?"

"I forgot," she replied, feeling like an idiot. No wonder the boat had moved backward when she'd turned the engine off. She imagined what would have happened if she'd rammed the throttle down. She'd have jerked the whole back end off the boat. "I didn't damage the motor or the boat, did I?"

"I doubt it." Stuart pressed the button to raise the anchor. He heard a twanging noise as the anchor rope became taut, and he removed his finger from the button. Slowly shifting the boat into reverse, he said, "We're hung up."

Her worried frown was replaced by a bright smile. The thought of being stranded on the lake with Stuart had a certain appeal now that she was beginning to come to terms with the idea of making love without being in love. Wasn't being stranded on a deserted island with a gorgeous hunk a common female fantasy?

"Why are you grinning?" Stuart asked, bewildered by her reaction. He shifted the throttle to the idle position.

"I was thinking about being stranded on a deserted island," she blurted out candidly.

Stuart felt his heart lurch in his chest. His hands clenched on the steering wheel. He could make her fantasy a reality. "I can get the anchor up," he said hoarsely, giving her a choice.

"Do you need help?" Elaine offered after a brief pause.

Fear had raised its ugly head when she'd considered what would happen if she told him not to bother with the anchor. Within seconds they'd both be shedding their scant clothing. Should they eventually make love, she didn't want to have to be a contortionist. She had enough to worry about without the awkwardness of elbows and knees bumping together.

"No, thanks." He'd given her a choice, and he had to accept her decision, but that knowledge didn't keep him from grinding his teeth in frustration. He moved to the back of the boat and tugged on the anchor rope. "On second thought, slide over and push the button that has a picture of the anchor on it, would you?"

"Okay." Elaine followed his directions, quickly finding the right button and pressing it. "Is it free?"

Yanking on the rope, Stuart felt the anchor relinquish its hold on whatever it had been caught on. He waited until he heard it lock into place and then said, "Yes."

"Good."

Stuart watched her move gracefully back to her seat, wondering what she thought was *good*—getting the anchor loose or postponing what he hoped was inevitable. Both, he silently gritted, feeling acute frustration.

Returning to the controls, he forced his facial muscles to lift the corners of his mouth to mask his inner turmoil.

On the way back to the boathouse he cursed his vivid imagination as graphic pictures in glorious Technicolor of what could have happened played in his mind. One thing was for certain, he mused: doing the right thing didn't hold a candle to giving in to the oldest temptation known to man. At least Adam had the tangy taste of apple juice in his mouth when he was cast out of the Garden of Eden.

"Apples to ashes," Stuart murmured astutely, shrewd enough to realize that indulging in temporary gratification would leave the taste of ashes in his mouth—and result in Elaine crossing him off her list permanently.

He'd asked Elaine to learn to trust him; he had to trust his own intuition. She had to get to know him before she could love him. Promising himself she'd have a clear picture of who and what he was, he rammed the throttle forward.

Elaine propped her feet on the bottom drawer of her desk and toyed with the pencil she'd been using to make notations. Daydreams, not fatigue, had distracted her the entire day. Over and over she'd replayed everything Stuart had said and done during the past twenty-four hours. She edited some of her reactions and intricately embellished others.

In particular she elaborated on what had happened at the end of the evening. In actuality he'd kissed her on the forehead and said good-night. Elaine, a person who preferred glorious happy endings, changed what had happened into what she *wished* had happened. His platonic kiss on the forehead was replaced by sizzling, lingering, passionate kisses. His tender farewell was exchanged for heartfelt vows of love and eternal devotion.

Elaine tapped the eraser end of her pencil against her upper lip. Daydreams aren't hazardous to my health, she reassured herself. Considering the fact that she hadn't fallen asleep until dawn and had been wide-awake when she'd opened the clinic at eight, she was beginning to think the additional adrenaline her daydreams had generated must be good for her.

Tracing the eraser tip over the curve of her lip, she chuckled aloud. She couldn't kid herself into believing fatigue wouldn't catch up with her. Come five o'clock she'd be yawning. By nine she'd be comatose.

She glanced at the phone. Would he call? Sandwiched between her daydreams, she must have silently asked herself that question a hundred times. The few times the phone had rung she'd nearly knocked Claire over in her rush to answer it. He hadn't called...yet. But she knew deep down in her heart that he would.

"Express delivery for you," Claire said, striding into Elaine's office and dropping a brown envelope on her desk.

One look at the return address brought a mile-wide smile to Elaine's face. Disregarding the staples, she yanked at the flap until the envelope was torn open.

"Who's it from?" Claire inquired, plopping into a chair and struggling to keep a straight face. Her jaw moved fast and furious as she chewed her gum for all it was worth. Elaine's behavior the entire day had been unusual. She acted as though she'd been given a treasure map and wasn't going to share the information. Claire was dying to know what was inside the brown wrapper.

"It's professional materials, I imagine," Elaine replied in an offhand manner, knowing full well that Claire had read the return address. Her hunch was confirmed when she heard Claire's gum pop in rapid succession like a gangster's machine gun.

Feigning innocence, Claire asked, "Something you ordered?"

"Hmm."

"I read the return address. Since when is Dr. Stuart Cimarron sending you reading material?"

Stuart's picture fell on the desk's top as Elaine shook the envelope. Claire pounced on it before Elaine could react. Pretending a nonchalance her pounding heart denied, Elaine slowly extracted the remaining contents of the envelope.

"What is it?" Claire demanded. Rising and circling the desk, she dropped the picture and peered over Elaine's shoulder.

"A résumé."

"Why would he send you his résumé? Why didn't you say something to me about expanding your services to include dental care as part of the prenatal package?"

Elaine opened her mouth to answer, but she wasn't quick enough. As usual, Claire promptly supplied the answers to her own questions.

"Actually, that's a brilliant idea. Let the ob-gyns top that one."

"I don't think that's why Stuart sent his résumé."

Elaine flipped through the pages and chuckled. Everything was there: a fact sheet, a photograph and a list of personal references. Her chuckle turned to laughter when she noticed the only woman's name listed was his sister's.

"What's so funny?" Claire snatched at the papers but missed. "You know, you're extremely reticent when it comes to Dr. Cimarron."

Elaine quickly answered the question before Claire could draw her own conclusions. "Stuart's clever way of letting me get to know him. We went to Annette's house for dinner last night. Later, after he'd taken me to Margery's house for an emergency call, we went for a late night swim."

"Ahhh."

Unlike the I-don't-know-anything noise Elaine had made earlier, Claire's "Ahhh" was stretched out and made her sound as though she knew everything. Elaine watched as Claire plucked a tissue from the box on her desk, wrapped her gum in it and deposited it into the wastebasket. She sat on the edge of the desk and sluggishly swung her leg back and forth.

"That explains why you've been starry-eyed and discombobulated today." She folded her arms across her chest. "I'm officially on strike until you tell me what's going on between you and the good dentist."

"What can I say other than I'm attracted to a nice guy?"

"That'll do for beginners. I gather you kept the promise you made to yourself?" Claire asked, concerned about Stuart's reaction to discovering why Elaine had chosen midwifery as a career.

"I told him that I was divorced and why." Elaine dropped into her chair. "He knows I can't have children."

"You told him?" Her blue eyes glowed with admiration for her boss. "Most women would have waited until the guy was madly in love and ready to propose before they told him. How'd he react?"

"At first he was stunned. When I asked him if he'd become involved with a woman who couldn't conceive, he didn't know what to say. He'd never been faced with a similar problem."

"Did you give him the specifics of your medical history? Women who've had a tubular pregnancy have been known to have babies. The odds are cut in half, but getting pregnant is still possible."

Elaine shook her head. "In my case, the chances are slim to none. Believe me, I did everything humanly possible to get pregnant. I'm not going to build false hopes by spouting statistics. I told Stuart there was a fertility problem—mine—and my ex-husband wanted children. When the bedroom became a battlefield, we mutually decided to end the marriage."

"When did you tell Stuart? At the door after a good-night kiss?"

"No. As a matter of fact, I told him on the way back to Annette's cabin."

Claire grinned. "I knew there was a reason I liked that man. You were completely straightforward, and he was smart enough not to let infertility become an insurmountable barrier. He's quite a guy, isn't he?''

"Yeah. Quite a guy."

Elaine would have lapsed into another daydream if Claire hadn't waved her hand within inches of her nose. Unfolding her arms, Claire hopped off the desk and briskly rubbed her hands together.

"The strike is over. Since you're out in la-la land, I'd better get to work. I'll collate the printed materials on breast-feeding and put them in packets for you." Claire strode toward the door, chuckling with glee. She hesitated, then pivoted on one foot. "Incidentally, boss, congratulations. You deserve the best."

Grinning, Elaine propped her elbows on her desk and stared at Stuart's picture. Usually she preferred informal snapshot photographs over professional portrait photographs, but whoever had taken this picture had captured Stuart's personality. His dark eyes sparkled with contained mirth, his crooked smile expressed his enjoyment of life's little pleasures.

She turned the picture over and read the message he'd written on the back. Her eyes narrowed as she tried to guess what the cryptic note meant. Last night at the lake, he'd used the lyrics of a song to prove a point. She silently sang the words of ''Tea for Two'' to herself. When she reached the last lines, her jaw dropped. Until now, the question she'd asked him regarding her infertility had gone unanswered. The lyrics of the song ''Tea for Two'' explicitly revealed how Stuart felt about children. He wanted two children: a boy and a girl.

Inwardly recoiling, she searched for a reasonable explanation other than the obvious one. Give him the benefit of the doubt. In his haste to get the package to her, he might have jotted the song title without giving the lyrics a second thought.

Her own insecurities wouldn't accept the weak explanation. Clamping her teeth on her bottom lip, she dropped his picture.

No, she silently told herself, Stuart was being as honest and blunt as she'd been. She'd told him she wouldn't seriously date a man without his knowing the truth. She had his answer.

Both she and Claire had been mistaken in believing that her inability to have children was unimportant to Stuart. A tremor ran through her as she returned his résumé and picture to the envelope. Slowly, as though it weighed a ton, she lifted the envelope. She opened her filing cabinet and shoved the envelope back into the dark recesses.

You'll be okay, she silently promised herself, moving toward the reception area. She blinked her eyes to clear her vision. Better to know now than later.

Determined not to dwell in a fantasy world that could only lead to heartache, she straightened her shoulders and marched toward Claire.

Glancing up from the stacks of printed material, Claire asked, "What's up?"

"Nothing, Claire. Absolutely nothing. Business as usual."

Chapter Six

Tammy Glenn listlessly shifted the bedcovers aside as Trey, her husband, ushered Elaine into the bedroom.

"Don't get up, Tammy." It was long past noon, but knowing night feedings could interrupt a mother's sleep, Elaine wasn't overly concerned.

The combination of not having heard from Tammy for several days and the underlying note of panic Elaine had heard in Trey's voice when he'd called was the reason behind her unscheduled visit. Trey was concerned about his happy, well-adjusted wife turning into an irritable shrew.

Elaine put her satchel on the foot of the bed, planning her nursing strategy. First she'd assess Tammy's physical condition. If her vital signs were normal, she'd consider a malady common to women who'd recently given birth: postpartum blues.

"I was checking on another patient and thought I'd drop in and see how you're feeling."

"I should have called you earlier this week, but..." Tammy sluggishly slid her feet out from under the covers and shrugged, unable to decide on a plausible excuse for her laziness. Unwelcome tears filled her eyes. "Trey called you, didn't he?"

"He's concerned about you," Elaine replied, neither confirming nor denying Tammy's suspicions. "I checked the baby before I came in to see you. She's beautiful."

"She's lost weight." Tammy self-consciously put her hand on one breast. "Maybe my milk isn't rich enough."

"It's normal for a baby to lose about ten percent of its body weight the first week or two," Elaine said reassuringly.

"But she cries."

Elaine watched Tammy swipe at the tear rolling down her cheek. She moved to sit beside her on the bed. Encouraging Tammy to use her shoulder to cry on, Elaine put her arm around her shoulders while inconspicuously placing her fingers over the pulse point on Tammy's wrist. From what she'd seen and heard, Tammy's symptoms were classic: irritability, indecisiveness and exhaustion. Her pulse was steady, but her emotional barometer was shaky.

A wry smile Tammy was unable to see twisted Elaine's mouth into a grimace. Both the new mother and the midwife shared a common ailment. She'd had the blues herself for the past few weeks. Unlike the woman softly sobbing in her arms, Elaine didn't have a darling baby to fill her lonely hours. Instead of the gurgling laughter of a baby to comfort her, Bob York's rendition of a tap dancer's tune had haunted her. Inside her head, the lyrics of "Tea for Two" played as though the needle were stuck on a crack in a phonograph record.

Silently shaking off the troublesome refrain, she threaded her fingers through Tammy's hair. "Are you having problems with breast-feeding?"

"No," Tammy gulped, slowly recovering from her bout of tears. "Sometimes they're tender, but I guess that's normal."

"Lie back. Let me see if there's a reason for the tenderness."

Tammy unbuttoned the front of her gown, unclasped the front of her maternity bra and pulled the cloth aside. With a clinical eye, Elaine methodically checked each breast while asking, "Any discomfort while nursing?"

"Uh-uh." Tammy turned her head aside and re-buttoned her gown. "Two weeks after the baby was born, my mother had to go home. Trey's mother came to help out, and she's against breast-feeding. She told me it was bovine in this day and age."

"There's nothing stupid about breast-feeding. Formula cannot duplicate breast milk. You have to remember that when Trey's mother was pregnant the fashionable way to feed a child was from a bottle. Today, the medical profession heartily endorses breast-feeding."

"She said it was such a pity that Trey couldn't share the wonder of being able to feed his son."

"Fathers don't express their love for a child by putting a bottle in the baby's mouth," Elaine countered, wondering what other wonderful tidbits Mrs. Glenn had dropped while "helping" her daughter-in-law. "That isn't really what's bothering you, is it?"

A single tear trickled from the corner of Tammy's eye and ran toward her ear. "No. Mother Glenn said..." She sniffed. "She said I'd lose my shape, and...maybe Trey, too."

Elaine leaned toward Tammy, putting one hand on the pillow beside Tammy's head. Well-meaning advice concerning pregnancy, natural childbirth and nursing was often based on false information, myths and prejudice. Her voice was quiet, calm, but inside she was seething. The gag law used in courtrooms to silence disorderly defendants was a good idea, Elaine fumed. She wished she was allowed to muzzle Mrs. Glenn.

"Remember how you fussed and grumbled the last month of your pregnancy?" Elaine asked in a tranquil voice that hid her inner turmoil.

Tammy nodded, hesitantly. "I thought I'd never be a size ten again."

"How many pounds have you lost?"

"Eighteen. But, I...my..." Her hands made sagging motions beneath her breasts. "What difference does it make what size I am if I have to lift my boobs to buckle my belt?"

In other circumstances, Elaine would have chuckled at Tammy's attempt at humor. Aware that this wasn't a laughing matter, in spite of Tammy's flippant remark, Elaine shook her head. "With a proper diet and exercise, you don't have to worry."

"You're sure?"

"Positive. Everything you're feeling is absolutely normal." She reached to the end of the bed, opened her medicine bag and pulled out a package wrapped in stork-covered paper. "I brought you a gift."

"Elaine, you shouldn't have," Tammy said, her eyes alight with pleasure. She took the box, neatly removed the bow, then tore the paper off. "What is it?"

"A diary of a woman who'd had her child naturally. Afterward, she had some of the same doubts you're having." Elaine grinned. "This woman had an older sister who spread the same myths Mrs. Glenn told you."

Tammy grabbed Elaine and gave her a mighty hug. "You're so good to me."

"You be good to yourself. Stop listening to other people and listen to your husband. Trey loves you. He's proud of you and his daughter. You need to say that—out loud—to keep everything in perspective. Think positively!"

"I know he loves me." Tammy flipped the cover open and read aloud the personal message Elaine had written. "In every generation there are a few women who are gifted with the ability to see beyond the popular beliefs of their time. These women are rare. They give all of us the freedom to experience new dimensions of perception. You and the author of this book have this gift . . . share it with those who are unafraid to see." Her eyes grew misty. "Thanks, Elaine. You, too, are a rare, gifted woman."

Elaine smiled. "We're turning into a mutual admiration society, aren't we?"

Their laughter brought Trey to the doorway. "Everything better?" he asked, unsure if he'd be welcome in the room.

"Come here and give your wife a hug and a kiss," Tammy invited, opening her arms wide.

Moving aside to make room for Trey, Elaine gathered her belongings. "Don't bother showing me to the door." Recalling having said those same words to Trey the morning his daughter had been born, she added, "I mean it. Your wife has something she wants to share with you."

The Tyler city limits sign was several blocks behind Elaine before she realized visiting Tammy had been just the tonic she'd needed to lift her spirits. She'd been preoccupied with her personal problems with Stuart.

Each day since she'd received his package, she'd awakened feeling depressed. He'd called frequently the first week. Claire had faithfully written down his number and handed it to her. As the days had passed, the calls had come less often. Elaine had finally realized that she'd been avoiding answering the phone for reasons other than playing hard to get. For once in her life, Claire didn't pry. The messages Stuart left with Claire remained on Elaine's desk unanswered. Elaine knew what he wanted without talking to him.

"Friendship," she muttered, steering into the parking lot beside the clinic. Her feelings were too intense for a platonic relationship. "Forget Stuart Cimarron. Concentrate on your work."

She barely had her foot in the door of the clinic when Claire shouted, "Telephone, Elaine. It's Johnny."

Picking up the extension in her office, Elaine said, "Hi, Johnny. How are you and Annette doing?"

"Fine. Annette asked me to call and invite you to a Fourth of July celebration here."

"I'd love it," Elaine replied. She'd dreaded spending the holiday alone. "Can I bring anything?"

"Wait a minute. I'll ask Annette."

Although Johnny put his hand over the receiver, Elaine could hear him mumble, "Don't know why I have to make the calls. Every time I end up relaying messages." In a louder voice, he called, "Annette, sweetheart, can Elaine bring anything?"

Elaine heard Annette's response in the background. "Stuart."

"My wife says you can bring Stuart if you like. Or I'll call Stuart and ask him to pick you up on his way out here."

Elaine paused, contemplating the consequences. Dodging Stuart's call was pointless if she allowed Johnny to make arrangements for her. Her mind raced, searching for a reasonable excuse.

"Holidays are notorious for being responsible for emergencies," she replied, utilizing the first excuse she could think of. "This time I think I'd better drive."

Elaine heard an extension on their end of the line being lifted.

"Hi, Elaine."

Johnny groaned aloud. "If you wanted to talk to her, why didn't you place the call? Annette, I'm going out to the shop. You make the rest of the calls. Bye, Elaine.''

"Bye, Johnny. See you Monday." She heard the receiver click and asked, "Why did you have him call?"

"Well," Annette responded, stringing out the word, "I wanted you to come to the get-together Monday, so I had my charming husband call. Invitations from him are tough to refuse. Speaking of men who are tough to refuse, Stuart says where you're concerned he's suffering from a bad case of halitosis. I hope halitosis isn't in the genes."

Chuckling, Elaine quipped, "Bad breath isn't hereditary. You're safe."

"Whew! That's a relief. I think it's affecting Stuart's sense of humor."

"Oh, yeah? How?"

"I put his receptionist, June, up to buying a giant economy-size bottle of mouthwash and leaving it on his desk. Stuart wasn't amused. He wanted to shout at me, but I reminded him of my present condition. He immediately calmed down."

Determined to circumvent Annette's curiosity about what she'd done to make Stuart short-tempered, Elaine inquired, "Can I bring a covered dish? Potato salad? Deviled eggs?"

"A couple of bags of chips and a dip would be helpful. Uh, I don't suppose Johnny happened to mention that Stuart will be here on the Fourth, too."

"Yes, he mentioned that he was supposed to call Stuart."

"You don't mind?"

"We're both civilized adults. I'm certain we can meet socially without causing a scene." Pride forced her to add, "I won't treat him any differently than your other male guests."

She wouldn't allow herself to go all weak-kneed and calf-eyed because of him. Absolutely not, she silently promised. She'd be calm and serene—at least on the outside, where it counted.

"Stuart won't like that treatment. He may appear civilized but I'm here to tell you that with provocation he can come unraveled at the seams just like any other mortal male." Annette chuckled at the prospect of watching her brother being bewitched by a woman who didn't return his sentiments. Too often his relationships with females had been the other way around. "It's good for him. He needs somebody to knock him back on his heels for a change."

"I hate to disappoint you, but I'm not the cause of whatever is bothering Stuart."

"Ha!" Annette chirped merrily. "Don't kid yourself. You've got him going wild. Believe me, no woman has ever ignored Stuart. In fact, I can't remember a time when he's had to do more than crook his little pinkie in a woman's direction to have her eating out of his hand. You've got him calling you!"

"He wants to be friends, that's all." Elaine made a sharp chopping motion with one hand. Annette's stubborn determination to play matchmaker drove Elaine to issue a none-too-subtle warning. "Hunting season is open on cupids. One of us, Stuart or myself, will shoot you the moment we hear angel's wings flapping. Understand?"

"My, oh, my!" Annette teased. "I hear a strange noise coming over the telephone wires. Is it the sound of your seams unraveling?"

Convincing Annette was impossible, Elaine decided, so she gave up trying. Annette could hear her, but she might as well be speaking a foreign language. Nothing registered that wasn't what she wanted to hear.

"The sound you hear after the click is the dial tone. I'll see you on the Fourth of July. Bye."

Despite the stouthearted proclamation Elaine had made to Annette and the pep talk she'd given herself as she'd dressed to get ready for the Fourth of July party, when she glanced toward the fragrant smoke billowing from the barbecue grill and saw Stuart, her knees weakened.

He was dressed in white shorts and a turquoise pullover shirt that accentuated his dark coloring and tan, and Elaine felt helplessly drawn in his direction. A tall chef's hat perched precariously on his head begged her hands to straighten it before it fell to the ground. Elaine's fingertips tingled in response to the mental image of feeling the texture of his hair as she righted the hat squarely on the crown of his head. She fanned her face with her hand in response to the flaming sensation.

Forcing herself to take a deep breath and relax, she rehearsed what she'd say to him. She'd tell him about Margery deciding to take Celeste and Sally to him for dental care. They'd talk about Annette's progress. Johnny's next pottery show was a safe topic. She'd be friendly and nice, with the emphasis on the latter. No matter what happened, she wouldn't be too friendly.

She didn't want him to think she'd come to the party to stalk him. Except for his sister and her husband and Margery Clements, they had few acquaintances in common. On rare occasions they'd meet socially, but she'd decided to make certain it didn't appear as though she were arranging the meetings.

The celebration had been in full swing when she'd arrived. Kids splashed in the lake; their parents visited back and forth while keeping an eye on them. Elaine heard a cluster of men discussing the price of commodities while their wives chatted about the children's latest stunts. Johnny and Annette mingled among their guests, socializing, unaware of her arrival.

As she tried to decide which way to go, toward the dock or into the cabin, she realized she'd hesitated too long. Hat in hand, Stuart parted the crowd, heading straight toward her.

"Can I take those?" he asked, pointing to the bags of potato chips she'd squashed against her breasts.

His dark eyes met hers. The questions they silently asked had nothing to do with potato chips, but they did cause a tingling sensation beneath the packages.

"No, thanks. I'll put them in the kitchen."

"I insist," he murmured, removing them from her hands.

Her heart sank when he turned away from her. He paused, pivoted and asked, "How are you at grilling hot dogs and chicken?"

"Inexperienced," she replied truthfully.

"There's no time like the present to learn. I've charred three packages of wieners. You can't possibly do any worse than I have." He waved toward the grill. "After you."

Casually, oh, so casually, she managed to put one foot in front of the other without stumbling. He was following her. She imagined she could feel his warm breath flowing over the back of her neck, soothing her as effortlessly as he'd once done with his hands.

Talk, she silently prompted herself. Do what you bragged to Annette that you could do. Be civilized!

"So," she began when they were standing next to each other at the grill. "How are you?"

Sick at heart, Stuart responded silently, wishing some scientific genius would invent a drug to relieve the shortness of breath he felt when he was near Elaine. Unless he got control of himself, he'd be panting after her in no time flat.

"Is that a medical question or a social inquiry?" he bantered, camouflaging his doubts and fears with humor.

"Social."

"Hmm." He picked up a long-handled fork and turned a row of wieners over. "Great. Burned on the outside, raw on the inside."

"Kids don't care," Elaine responded, refusing to consider the possibility that his words had a hidden meaning. She pulled a bun from the cart beside the grill and held it open. "Plenty of mustard and ketchup will disguise anything."

Stuart forked a wiener into the bun and watched as Elaine liberally applied squirts of bright yellow mus-

tard over the blackened part. He made a comical face
as she poured an equal amount of ketchup over the
mustard.

"Taste test," she remarked, lifting the hot dog to
her mouth. She licked a dribble of mustard from the
bun, then took a big bite. She chewed the awful wiener gamely, then swallowed. She set the hot dog aside,
knowing her stomach would openly revolt at the
thought of having to digest food while twisted into a
million tiny knots. "The kids will love them."

"Care to try the chicken?" he asked, amusement
making his eyes dance merrily.

"I don't think it's done."

Stuart turned a thigh over. Unlike the wieners, it
wasn't burned to a crisp. "How can you tell?"

"Stick it with the fork. If the juice looks pink, it's
still raw."

Stuart placed the long-handed fork at the juncture
of his hand and wrist. Meaningfully he said, "Raw."

"You look good enough to eat," Elaine blurted out
without thinking. Stuart's dark eyes snapping hungrily in her direction made her want to crawl under the
picnic table and pull the tablecloth over her. Or better
yet, squirt mustard and ketchup on herself to thoroughly disguise herself before she disappeared under
the table.

"You're delectable, too." Stuart's glib response was
accompanied by his heart-stopping smile.

At least she doesn't think I'm ugly, he mused, his
hopes kindling. Must be another reason she didn't return my calls. What? Was it something he'd said,
something in the résumé, that had offended her?

Dammit, the invitation he'd hurriedly written on the back of the picture was old-fashioned enough for a Victorian miss. *Tea for Two* couldn't possibly be misconstrued as *Let's Get Physical*.

"How's business? Margery told me Celeste and Sally are insisting that you be their dentist," Elaine babbled, resorting to the canned spiel she'd practiced in the hope of muzzling her impetuous mouth.

"I'm seeing them next week." Stuart doused a blue flame licking the underside of a chicken breast with water. "How about you?"

"Business as usual. One delivery last month."

"Annette is into her fifth month and she's still flitting around as though she had ants in her pants," Stuart grumbled disapprovingly. "Can't you get her to slow down?"

"No. Furthermore, I wouldn't ask her to curtail her normal activities. Midwives don't interfere with what comes naturally for a patient." His sister was energetic, a fireball. To impose rigid constraints on her would be like attempting to harness a hummingbird. "She's become a voracious reader. Half of my library on natural childbirth is here. Unless she can read and flit around at the same time, I'd say she's moderated her activities."

Elaine took one last close-up glance at Stuart. She'd used up her entire supply of chitchat. She'd been cordial. Although reluctant to move away from him, she had to be strong—for both of them, if necessary.

"I haven't had a chance to say hello to Johnny and Annette." She stood on tiptoe and glanced around the crowded lawn. More guests had arrived, but she'd been too engrossed by Stuart to notice. Walk away, she ordered herself firmly. Just smile and get the hell away from him. "It's been nice talking to you. Good luck with the chickens."

Short of reaching out and physically grabbing her arm, Stuart was at a loss as to how to keep her by his side. She'd turned and weaved her way through several couples before her name slipped from between his lips.

"Elaine."

She turned, glad to be at the perimeter of the magnetic force field that radiated around Stuart. Two steps, she thought, maybe three, and I'll be able to resist the pull.

"Yes?"

"I waited for your call." She moved toward him lethargically, as if she had no will of her own. His voice dropped to an intimate level when he asked, "Elaine, why didn't you call? What did I do that's so utterly unforgivable?"

"I read what you wrote on the back of your picture."

"'Tea for Two'?" he said, sincerely puzzled. "Is that something obscene?"

"No, but you're a man who listens to lyrics. The last sentence of the song was your reply to the question I'd asked. I couldn't see any future in—"

Stuart dropped the fork he'd held and grasped her arms: his fingers bit into her soft flesh. "The song title was an invitation, not a declaration of intent."

Elaine's jaw dropped open, then closed. Aware she must resemble a fish out of water, she whispered, "But the song mentions having children."

Comprehension struck Stuart like a thunderbolt. "Shut up," he ground out fiercely. In broad daylight, in front of three-fourths of the town's population, he hauled her against his chest and buried his face in her hair. "I misunderstood what you meant twice, but I gave you a chance to explain. Dammit, Elaine. You've got my receptionist ready to quit because I've snapped at her. My sister has threatened to keep my unborn niece or nephew isolated from me until I get a civil tongue in my head. Hell's bells, woman, if I owned a dog I'd have teeth marks up and down both legs."

He was holding her so tightly she thought her ribs would crack. He spoke softly, rapidly, as though physically holding her wasn't enough to keep her in his arms. His fingers held her face against his neck. Her lips could feel his pulse racing like a wild thing.

The particular song title he'd chosen was a Freudian slip, her mind warned her. Consciously, it was an invitation, subconsciously, it told you he wants a family. Listen to what his heart says, not his mind.

"Stuart, please, I promised Annette we wouldn't cause a scene."

His hands slipped from her waist to the back pockets of her shorts, molding her closer to him, refusing to release her. "No. The minute you're at a safe distance from me, you'll lower your emotional thermostat to subzero. I won't let you freeze me from your life. Right now I can feel your body radiating heat through your clothing. As long as I'm touching you, it's impossible to revert back into a block of ice, isn't it?''

Out of the corner of her eye Elaine saw a woman nudge her husband with her elbow. Both of them stopped their conversations and stared at her openly. Inwardly shuddering, Elaine realized that by ten o'clock the entire county would be buzzing with gossip.

Her face flamed, partially from embarrassment and partially from anger. She lifted her foot and placed her heel on the laces of his tennis shoes. Softly, sweetly, she asked, "How'd you like to have a fallen arch?''

"Threats won't work," he replied succinctly.

Elaine raised her arm and waggled her fingers. "See these fingers? Ever been pinched by a duck?''

He shouldn't have laughed, but he couldn't help it. "Do it," he told her brashly. His black eyes sparkled with contained mirth as he said, "Remember Annette accusing me of going around saying quack, quack? You'll just be giving me a legitimate excuse to take off my shirt and walk around going 'Quack, quack.' ''

"You're too conservative to pull a prank like that," Elaine said, calling his bluff. Her fingers dropped to his waist.

"Conservative? As in staid? Stuffy? Sweetheart, I'm a changed man since I visited the Mother's Clinic. Until then I seldom raised my voice or snapped at a woman."

She moved her hands to his chest, arched her back and pushed. Her efforts to break his hold were unsuccessful. "Don't blame me, Dr. Cimarron. We both know how everyone will construe your strutting around making duck noises. They'll think you're expressing your professional opinion of midwives.''

"Maybe. That's a risk you'll be taking if you pinch me." His voice dropped, becoming serious. "There's only one way you're going to get released from my clutches.''

"Name it," she sputtered.

"You're going to listen to what I have to say. You can either let the rest of this fair county hear my explanation...or you can walk down to the lake with me, find a solitary spot and hear me out." He nodded his head to one side. "A crowd is going to form at any minute. You have five seconds to decide. One... two...''

"Aren't you being a bit high-handed? I could just open my mouth and scream my head off.''

"Then you'll be the one making the explanations. Three...''

"Now I understand why your sister pretends to listen to your advice and then does as she damned well pleases.''

"Two..." He kept his voice steady, oblivious to the rising panic he heard in hers. "One...''

"Okay. You win. But I'm warning you up front— you won't convince me that your choice of songs wasn't a Freudian slip.''

His eyes narrowed at her final remark, his hands dropped to his sides. "Turn around and march," he commanded quietly. "I'll be right behind you.''

Glaring at him, she straightened her shoulders, pasted a social smile on her face and followed his orders. His blaming her for being the cause of his unusual behavior had wounded her pride, making her rebellious. His accusing her of changing him from a sane, rational man to one who snapped at his sister and employees was grossly unjust. She'd hear him out, but that didn't mean she'd be convinced. He'd overpowered her, but she was still in control of the situation.

Mentally backtracking, she wondered if she *was* in control. She was two feet ahead of him, and yet she could still smell the pleasant mixture of soap and hickory smoke on his skin. The faint salty taste of his skin lingered on her lips. Her hands could feel the soft texture of the shirt that had clung to his solid chest as she'd pushed against him. Yes, her mind rebelled against Stuart Cimarron's high-handedness, but her senses of smell, taste and touch were traitors.

Head down, she picked her way along the edge of the lake. The sounds of music and laughter faded with each step. "Over there," she heard from behind. Her eyes followed the direction of his finger. The shoreline jutted out, and several boulders lined the water's edge. The one closest to the water flattened out like a natural dock.

She refused his help when he crossed in front of her, lithely jumped on a large rock, turned and offered his hand. When he hopped to the next boulder, she scrambled up the first one. She'd demonstrate her independence. She could, literally and figuratively, make it on her own. It wasn't easy, but she could do it.

By the time she reached the flat boulder, Stuart had stretched out on his back with his hands pillowing his head. She crossed her legs and sat down Indian-style.

He rolled onto his side and propped his head in his hand. "First, I'll apologize for my uncouth behavior at Annette's party. It wasn't premeditated. I'd planned on cornering you and finding out what had gone wrong, but my strategy didn't include manhandling or embarrassing you."

Elaine sealed her lips, neither accepting nor refusing to accept his apology. She wrapped her arms around her legs and stubbornly rested her chin on her knees. She stared blindly at the water.

"Secondly, I rushed around like a chicken with its head cut off to get same-day delivery on the package you received." Realizing his chronological order was as jumbled as his untypical behavior, he said, "But let's go to back to the previous night. We agreed getting to know one another was more important than the explosive chemistry between us. When I kissed your forehead and departed, I decided the most expedient means for you to get to know me would be through a detailed résumé. I went home and started working on it. I haven't written one since I was in college, so it took several hours to complete."

Stuart couldn't read her mind to find out what she was thinking. He watched her face for a reaction to what he'd said. Her profile could have been carved in ivory for all the clues it gave. The breeze coming off the lake had blown a single strand of dark hair across her face, but she hadn't bothered to brush it aside. She wasn't giving his intuitive powers the slightest clues to what was going on in her mind.

"I'd had two hours sleep when I arrived at the office. I gave June the résumé to type while I made arrangements to have the package picked up and delivered out of town. At the last minute, I decided to enclose a picture. The deliveryman arrived while I was scrounging through my personal files, searching for something more formal than a snapshot. You probably noticed it wasn't a recent photograph.''

He waited for a nod or a verbal reply. He heard only the sound of boat motors coming from the main body of the lake and saw only the same masklike expression on her face.

Elaine felt the tension building in her shoulders and neck. His gift for speaking directly from the heart in a husky tone was affecting her willpower. Maintaining the appearance of being disinterested was becoming a chore that required every muscle and fiber in her body.

''The deliveryman was standing behind me, reading over my shoulder, practically breathing down my neck when I signed the picture and flipped it over to add a personal note. I felt like a kid who puts his hand over a test paper to keep a cheater from copying his work.'' He'd digressed, but he wanted Elaine to be aware of every minute detail that had influenced what he'd written. ''I sat there, racking my brain for inspiration. The deliveryman started humming along with music piped into the office.''

'' 'Tea for Two'?'' Elaine muttered.

''Yeah. I thought, why not? I could recall most of the lyrics.'' A wayward smiled tugged at his lips. ''Fate—and the impatient deliveryman—seemed to have stepped in to lend a helping hand. When I remembered the rendition our favorite musician played, that made the choice even better. I jotted down the song title, shoved the picture in the envelope and . . . you know the rest.''

She cocked her head in his direction. His explanation was plausible, but it dodged the issue. Elaine locked her arms tighter around her legs and asked, ''What about the last line of the song? We can't have children of either sex.''

Chapter Seven

For a lady who believes in letting nature take its course, you're wielding a mighty mean scalpel," Stuart commented, feeling as though she were preparing to perform surgery on him, cutting him out of her life permanently.

Elaine knew exactly what would happen if she let desire rule her mind: they'd be sharing a bed instead of a boulder.

"I don't take clients who are a medical risk," she replied. "My first and foremost concern is for the welfare of the woman and her unborn child. I want what's best for them."

"And you want what is best for us?" he countered.

"Yes." She unlocked her arms and straightened her legs, preparing to leave if he continued to shy away from answering her question. "We're headed toward a pointless dead-end relationship, one destined for heartache. I've been there once. I'd be a fool to ignore my medical history and topple into bed with you to temporarily fill an emotional void in my life."

"Temporary fillings do eliminate pain until a permanent filling is affixed," Stuart rejoined thoughtfully.

"I'm a midwife, not a dentist. Temporary fillings are a waste of time and energy in this case." Elaine started to rise, but Stuart delayed her by circling his arms around her wrist. She heard his deep sigh of frustration. "We've talked. Let go, please."

"I can't let go. Don't you think I tried? Each time I called, I swore I wouldn't call again if you didn't respond. And yet I did."

Elaine knew how difficult letting go could be. It meant accepting defeat. Failure. She'd tried to avoid failure once by clinging to Joe, by building false hopes. The final outcome hadn't been changed by either tactic. She'd failed anyway.

Time and distance had given her a new perspective on letting go: It meant getting on with your life. That was exactly what she'd done, what Stuart would have to do. In time, she mused sadly, Stuart would forget her.

"Let go," she repeated quietly.

"No. I'm not giving up."

He tugged on her wrist until she collapsed next to him. Cupping her face in his hand, he gently turned her toward him. His eyes beseeched her to listen carefully. "I won't lie to you. Yes, I admit that until we met I considered marriage and family as synonymous. But your being unable to have children doesn't rule out raising a family."

"Adoption?"

"That's one choice."

"It takes years because of the waiting lists. I spent two years waiting, hoping, praying for a child." She withdrew his hand from her face and shook her head. "No."

"Surrogate mother?" he suggested.

"That's risky, too. You've read the newspapers. You know what can happen."

"I can't believe you're so pessimistic. You preach positive thinking to your patients, but you practice fatalism."

Elaine jumped to her feet and dusted off the back of her shorts as she said, "Don't confuse positive thinking with daydreaming, which is what you've been doing. You haven't made a choice. You've skirted around the issue, grasping at straws, seeking a means of postponing the inevitable."

"You're wrong." He stood, bodily blocking her path of escape. "I've done my homework."

"Meaning?"

"The books I read on infertility and divorce say divorced women who can't have children have received two psychological blows. Sometimes those women react by going on a sexual binge...and sometimes they're immobilized by a fear of future failures. I didn't think what I read applied to you, because you give the outward appearance of knowing who you are and where you're going. You're perpetrating a fraud, Elaine. Every objection you've given to the alternatives of having a child yourself is based on being too damned scared to take a risk."

"Psychological gibberish," Elaine retorted coolly. "I'm not afraid of taking risks. I'm the one who pulled up my roots from Tennessee and transplanted myself to North Carolina after my divorce. I'm the one who took the risk of opening a midwife clinic when I could have easily found work in a hospital maternity ward."

"Material risks," he said discounting her words. Pointing to her heart, he asked, "What about personal risk? How many men have you dated since you left Tennessee?"

"Not many, but—"

"Watch it," he warned when she swatted his hand. "You're going to give weak excuses, not valid reasons."

"Before you rudely interrupted, I was about to say that dating, or even going so far as to sleep with a man, doesn't prove anything. It doesn't take courage to have sex."

"It would for you. You said it yourself the night we were in the boat. Casual sex is repugnant to you, or words to that effect. Think about it, Elaine. What is the real reason you told me you couldn't have children?"

"I wanted to be fair. Hiding the truth would be deceitful."

"Admirable," he conceded, "but I think this matter goes deeper. Because you're scared, you purposely misread what I wrote on the back of the picture to mean that I wanted children. My note gave you an excuse to sever the relationship before you were forced to delve beyond the excuses you've come to believe, didn't it?''

"No." Then why hadn't she given him a chance to explain? Why did she avoid him? Elaine squeezed her eyes shut as though by doing so she wouldn't hear him answer his own question. She knew he wouldn't be satisfied with removing the decay, he was going straight to the root of the problem.

Intuitively he knew he'd struck a nerve, but he couldn't stop. He reached for her, giving her the comfort of having someone to lean on. In a barely audible voice, he asked, "Is it possible your past hurt and anger caused you to form some cockeyed notion that you aren't really a whole woman because you can't have children?''

"No." No? Maybe.

"Admit it, sweetheart. If not aloud, at least be truthful with yourself.''

Hard as she tried to deny what he'd said, she knew there were elements of truth in the conclusion he'd drawn. She'd bottled up the real reason and tried to ignore it for so long she'd almost forgotten it. She'd buried it beneath a pile of believable excuses: I don't want to be hurt, I don't want to be deceitful, I don't want to have casual sex.

Stuart had cared enough to blast through the excuses she'd made and sift through the chaff until he'd found the truth. She shivered, not from cold or from being in Stuart's arms when she wanted to hide her head under her bedclothes but from the chilling fear that confronted her.

You're a lousy bed partner, Elaine Kramer.

Joe hadn't said those words, but he'd thought them when he'd blamed her for being unable to get pregnant. He'd stopped coming to her for pleasure. She couldn't satisfy him; he couldn't satisfy her. She began trembling uncontrollably as she stuck a label on her fear: frigid.

"Easy, sweetheart," Stuart crooned, feeling her muscles tense, her body shake. "Easy now. Can you tell me about it?"

"No!" she whispered. She would have twisted from his arms, but she wasn't sure she could stand alone. She clenched her jaw to keep her teeth from chattering.

"You'll feel better if you get it out of your system," he said encouragingly as guilt washed over him. By callously probing, he'd unlocked Elaine's private hell. Shock victims in trauma had the same physical symptoms. He wanted to blanket himself around her, to protect her, to keep her warm. Moving one arm beneath her knees, he lifted her, carrying her off the boulder to the privacy and seclusion provided by the trees. She was rigid in his arms, like a small child who'd been injured, too frightened to cling, and yet, too scared to let go. He eased her to the ground, then quickly lay beside her, holding her securely. Patches of sunlight dappled her skin, warming her. "It's going to be okay, sweetheart."

A strangled whimper came from deep in her chest. Her mind spun at a crazy pitch, bouncing from what had happened to what would happen if she dared to reveal her inner conflict. Her throat worked hard to swallow. Her fingers dug into Stuart's shoulders.

Unspoken questions pelted her with stinging intensity until she felt as if she were caught in a hailstorm. Why had she become frigid? Had she always been frigid? No, her mind recoiled. She'd felt true passion, true desire. Then when had it happened? Whose fault was it? Mine? His? Could she change? Would it be different with another man? When? With whom? Stuart? Stuart! He was holding her as though she were too precious to release. She had to know...had to find out. She knew it was wrong to use Stuart as a guinea pig, but she had to know the truth. Was she frigid?

Her arms locked around Stuart's neck. "Kiss me. Please, kiss me," she begged him fervently, hoping against hope to disprove her self-revelation.

Stuart instantly felt a change when her lips sought his. Her skin became hot, feverish. Her legs wrapped around his as she welded them together. Her torso twisted against him until her nipples tightened into hard pebbles.

Liquid fire, he thought as she drew his tongue deep into her mouth. He was being consumed by a driving force that resembled passion but wasn't. Knowing he was responsible for her turmoil and knowing he wanted her to ignite beneath his hands, he willingly surrendered to exculpate her fear.

He rotated her shoulders until her back was pressed into the pine needles. Her legs remained twined around his, pulling him with her, cradling him intimately. A double bolt of desire jolted through him when her hands crept beneath his shirt, touching his bare skin. Within the space of a heartbeat, his desire to comfort her changed to primitive male need. His mind no longer governed his actions; his control and self-restraint snapped. Abruptly his mouth turned savage with need.

Elaine opened her eyes when she felt her cotton top raised over her waist and breasts. Lifting her shoulders, she helped him remove it, then tossed it aside. His palm covered the underside of her swimsuit bra, her nipple budded between his spread fingers. He massaged her breast as thoroughly as he'd massaged her shoulders and neck on a previous occasion. His lips molded the lace to her skin as he brought the sensitive tip inside his mouth.

"Sweet," he murmured against her flesh, sending an electrical charge sizzling from his mouth downward. "I've laid awake at night dreaming of this. God, you feel so good."

His low, husky words, punctuated by fiery nibbles and moist kisses along the smooth skin of her breasts, spread streamers of desire through her, but the small analytical portion of her mind remained aloof, tormenting her with doubt. She hated comparing and contrasting Stuart's lovemaking with Joe's, but she couldn't help it.

She'd always loved being kissed and touched. Cuddling, the glorious prelude to lovemaking, had been absent during the last year of her marriage. While Stuart devoted his hands and mouth to awakening her desire, in the past Joe had forgotten the necessary prerequisites to attaining fulfillment.

Elaine saw Stuart's fingers tremble as they undid the front clasp of her bra. His dark eyes glowed with pleasure before he nuzzled one breast, then the other. She heard a low purring sound but couldn't be certain who was making it until she felt it resonating in the back of her throat, bursting out with a will of its own. Automatically her teeth clamped down on her lip.

In the past, lovemaking had been a silent affair. Joe hadn't spoken, nor had he wanted her to make unseemly noises that might have distracted him from his task of getting her pregnant.

"Don't hold back," Stuart urged. His hands continued their quest, defining the shape of her breasts, making them ache under the sensuous kneading as he moved his lips to hers. He kissed her until he felt her full lower lip relax. He kissed her eyes, the tip of her nose, the hollows of her cheeks. "You have to let me know how you like to be touched, sweetheart."

She uttered a small gasp of pleasure when his hand moved to her waist and around the slender curve of her hips, cupping her buttocks and firmly squeezing. How different, she mused, feeling the shadow of heat that remained where he'd touched her. Had she ever been stroked so thoroughly? She couldn't remember.

Her lips curved into a delicious smile when she became aware that the rational part of her mind wasn't functioning properly. Had she been compelled to continue dissecting every move Stuart made and compare it with those she'd experienced with Joe, she'd have known that a part of her heart still belonged to her ex-husband. She'd have had to stop

Stuart, or she'd have hated herself later for giving Stuart what belonged to another man.

Freedom coursed through her veins. Her self-esteem soared, making her feel light-headed. Joe was the forgotten past; Stuart was her future.

Her senses skittered wildly as she arched against him. She heard a low growl and felt his hand clench. He'd signaled what aroused him. She moved her hips, rubbing the double stitching of her shorts against his front.

"Ah, sweetheart, it's going to be too late to stop if you keep doing that." He held her motionless in the cradle of his pelvis. He groaned when he realized that it was already too late. He lowered her to nature's bed of pine needles and braced his arms on each side of her shoulders. He watched the emerald-green flicker of passion in her eyes. "I want you, Elaine. Here. Now."

A pine needle prickling through the backside of her shorts, and the loss of physical contact with Stuart, made her conscious of where they were. Gazing at Stuart's face, she saw evidence of what it cost him to give her a chance to refuse. Lines of tension marred his brow and cheeks.

"Take off your shirt and put it under me," she coaxed seductively.

Stuart whipped his shirt over his head and stretched it beneath her hips and legs. Aware that her bare shoulders were vulnerable, too, he retrieved her blouse and spread it under her head and shoulders. The tail of her blouse overlapped his shirt. He'd protected her from harm.

While he tended to her, she wrapped her arms around his waist, loving the feel of her bare skin against his. Sensations she'd locked in her memory guided her hands as she leaned back against her blouse. Stuart remained statuelike as her fingers daintily traced the hollow at the base of his neck. The dark, matted hair on his chest formed a V and vanished below his waistband. Her fingers unsnapped his shorts. Slowly she separated the Velcro strips. The weight of the coins in his pockets aided the pull of gravity. His shorts crumpled onto the ground beside her.

Elaine smiled. She'd seen magazine ads with sexy men in near-nothing bikini swim trunks, but none came close to comparing with Stuart. Gently she lowered the scanty swatch of material.

Simultaneously Stuart tucked his long fingers beneath the knit fabric of her shorts and tugged them over her hips and legs. In all his days he'd never seen a lovelier woman. Before straddling her, he swiftly discarded the remainder of his clothing. Careful to balance his weight on his elbows and knees, he prolonged the sweet ecstasy of touching her from head to toe.

For one agonizing second, Elaine remembered those exhausting sessions with Joe, gaining nothing, proving nothing except that in the final analysis the test results indicated she'd failed her husband again.

Stuart felt her tense. Concerned that he'd been selfish in wanting to sprawl across her, he asked, "Elaine? Am I too heavy, sweetheart?"

She locked her arms around his neck, fighting the unwelcome memory. Her knees closed on each side of his narrow hips to prevent him from pulling away.

"No," she managed to gulp.

Stuart brushed his lips back and forth against hers. Instinctively he knew she'd been fine until his weight had wedged them together. "What is it? Tell me."

"I can't," she whimpered. A blush of shame spread across her cheeks. She wanted to make love with him, needed to, but Lord have mercy, she was scared. Her eyes squeezed tightly shut. What if she couldn't please him? What if...

"I'll hold you. Just hold you," he promised, instantly worried that he'd gone beyond what she'd intended. "We don't have to make love, sweetheart."

"It isn't that I don't want to make love, it's..." Her voice dwindled. She inhaled and opened her eyes. His face hovered over hers, her hands raised to frame it. "I'm so damned scared."

Stuart turned his head until his lips touched her palm. He shifted his weight to his side, holding her loosely. "Of me?"

"No. Of myself. I mean..." How was she going to explain? She'd been married, she wasn't a reluctant virgin, for heaven's sake. Explanations began to form in her mind, but she rejected each of them as completely asinine.

"Slowly." He kissed the side of her face, then her ear and throat. Her wildflower fragrance blended with the tangy odor of crushed pine needles and dried leaves. His hand slithered from the erratic pulse beat in her neck to the cleft between her breasts. "There's nothing you can't share with me."

Elaine hesitated, then blurted her suspicions in a dry whisper. "I don't think I'll please you."

"You please me immeasurably. You're so soft, so vibrant, so warm." His hand trailed across her rib cage and down the sweet curve of her slender waist to the round flare of her hips. "You're a very desirable woman, Elaine Kramer. I love how your skin seems to burn with heat as I touch you."

She reached up to brush a dark lock of hair from his brow. "I'm not cold."

From the lack of inflection in her voice, Stuart couldn't tell whether she was asking a question or making a remark. Relying on his instincts, he said, "No, love, you aren't cold by any stretch of the imagination."

Her dark fringe of lashes widened until he could see her emerald-blue eyes, her dark pupils expanded as though to draw him inside her soul. Her endearing habit of chewing on her bottom lip when she was deep in thought brought a small smile to his mouth.

Without her making a sound, he knew the secret behind her withdrawal and her fluctuation between hot and cold. Somewhere she'd gotten the idea that she was incapable of creating or responding to passion.

He took her hand and placed it where his had been. "Feel the heat?"

"Yes..."

His hand guided hers down the length of his torso. "With each touch I feel as though you've kindled flames. Touch me, sweetheart. I want to feel the fire."

For long minutes, Elaine did as he asked. As though blind, she learned where and how to touch him, gauging the effect of her hands by his breathing and the guttural sounds in his throat.

Stuart could tell from the initial uncertainty of her first stroke that she hadn't really believed what he'd told her. It was only when she felt the building heat and saw his ready response that her hand became bolder. Her fingers singled out the sensitive erogenous zones of his body and caressed them with such loving attention that it made his eyes water. Stuart felt positive he was falling apart, limb by limb.

Unable to endure the sweet torment without shaming his masculinity, he pressed her back against her shirt. "No more, woman. I'm going to explode."

Elaine read his eyes. The light flickering inside him had nothing to do with devilishness or humor. It was passion. She could see it, smell it in the thin veil of perspiration coating his square jaw. Her tongue flicked out, she wanted his taste in her mouth to savor.

Confident her fears of ineptness had diminished, he bestowed long, lingering kisses and equally passionate caresses. To overcome her inhibitions he had to drive her beyond the brink of passion to euphoric rapture. "I'll make it happen," he promised fervently. "Trust me. Don't hold back."

Moaning, arching toward his hand, Elaine writhed as his hard fingers touched her. Her legs slid against his in a frenzy. She cried out, her voice raspy with need. His mouth closed over hers, drinking in the passion he'd given birth to.

"I want you, Stuart." Her hips moved against his with urgency as she tried assuage her aching need.

He pulled himself over her. Then, gripping her thighs with his hands, he drove into her so completely that he heard her moan of pleasure echo his own. Warm and willing, she sheathed him tightly.

She wrapped her long legs around his hips, setting the pace with the circular motion of her hips, driving him wild. His powerful thrusts ignited a wildfire that consumed both of them.

"Be mine, sweetheart," he whispered urgently. "Give me all of you." His darkly tanned face was rigid with desire as he watched the depths of her eyes become a glorious, brilliant emerald green. "Now."

She couldn't fight the tingling sensation that started at her toes and spiraled around the contracted muscles of her legs, hips and chest, peaking as her eyelids fluttered closed. Her lips parted. Her hands moved up his sleek biceps, her fingers dived into his damp hair and drew his mouth to hers. Greedily she opened her lips and kissed him wildly, swallowing his muffled groan as the sun exploded.

Consciously, Elaine knew she was lying flat on the ground. Subconsciously, she felt as though she were flying free, soaring to previously unattainable heights. Passion purified her, diluting her secret fear until it vanished completely. She knew what her patients felt during a "peak experience." Nothing she'd ever felt equaled it.

From eons away she heard his cry of triumph bonding with her spontaneous gurgle of laughter. Then she drifted slowly back to reality. It felt wonderful. She felt wonderful—sexy, womanly, fulfilled. Tears of joy welled up in her throat.

Replete, she lazily ran her toes over the hair on the backs of his legs. She combed the damp hair above his ears toward the back of his well-shaped head with the tips of her fingers. Smiling softly, she whispered, "Thank you."

Stuart sighed heavily, resting his head between her breasts, too lethargic to wonder who should be thanking whom. She'd taken him with such hunger that he felt completely devoured. Even the private niche hidden deep inside his being, his soul, had become a part of her. His hand grazed over his chest as he hoped she'd replaced it with her own.

He cradled her head on his shoulder as he shifted to his side. Faint rays of sunlight filtered through the canopy of branches and leaves overhead. Stuart blinked, not because of the sun's brightness but because of his sense of wonder as he accepted an irrefutable burst of enlightenment. He loved her.

He'd known from the beginning that he genuinely cared for Elaine Kramer. But when had he fallen in love? There had been a score of times when he'd felt a twinge in his heart, an awakening. His eyes closed, and a collage of mental pictures crowded together. Had it happened when he'd seen her reluctance to go along with the brotherly prank he'd played on his sister, when he'd first seen her tuck her bottom lip under that lovable, slightly crooked front tooth? Or had it happened when he'd watched her with Celeste and Sally on her lap? It could have been when her mobile face had openly expressed vulnerability. He couldn't pinpoint the exact moment it had happened, but that didn't alter the fact that he was totally, helplessly in love with her.

Elaine tilted her head and strung butterfly kisses across his chin. "You're wonderful," she whispered, openly giving him the accolade he so richly deserved. "I was married for years, but I've never experienced anything like that."

"Is that a smug note I hear in your voice?" he asked, lightly teasing the delicate skin beneath his hand.

"Definitely." Somewhere in the distance, Elaine heard a rooster crow. "Was that you?"

"Nope, but that's exactly what I'd do if I had the energy. Strut. Crow. Flap my arms." Instead, he stifled a yawn. "What I'd better do is get up and jump into the lake before I burrow deeper into this makeshift bed of ours and fall sound asleep for a century or two."

Elaine, on the other hand, felt like Rip Van Winkle when he'd awakened. Playfully she shook his shoulder. "Come on, Rip, it's lousy bedside manners to make love, then snore."

"I don't snore." He squinted through one eye at her. "Do you?"

"Like a tornado," she fibbed gamely. She reached beside him, gathering both pieces of her swimsuit. The thought of feeling the lake water rushing across her sensitized skin invigorated her. Seconds later she slipped the ties of her swimsuit over her shoulder. "Come on, lazybones. Last one in is a rotten...tooth!"

She knew that would get him. What dentist could resist such a taunt? As she rose, ready to dash into the water, she felt his hand circle her ankle, restraining her.

"You'd go off and leave me when I'm completely wrung out?" he asked. He managed to keep his devilish smile from stretching his mouth into a grin, but he was completely unable to stop it from reaching his eyes. He shook his head in mock sadness. "You're a heartless woman, Elaine Kramer."

"Yes," she replied, shaking her ankle loose. She *was* heartless—she'd given hers to him earlier.

Elaine's surefooted gait reflected the banishment of her inner conflict. Stuart had eliminated her secret fear that she might be frigid. Her wanton response to him left no doubt that she was well within the normal range sexually. She'd replaced her secret fear with a new, wonderful secret. Although she'd encouraged him to join her, she was happy to have a moment to hug herself and silently cherish her secret love.

Standing at the edge of the water, she tested the water with her toe. Delicious, she thought, anticipating the clean feeling of having it wash over her. She scanned the crystal-clear water in search of sunken boulders. Executing a shallow dive, she swam a couple of strokes, then stood waist-deep in water, lifting her face to let droplets stream down her back.

A rowdy whooping noise coming from behind her spun her around in time to see Stuart running toward the water. Completely uninhibited, he crooked his arms, flapped them and let out a bellow. "Whoooo-eeeee!"

She gasped when he plunged into the water next to her. He banded her waist with his hands and lifted her high. She flung her head back and circled his wide shoulders with her arms as he pivoted around and around.

"Don't dunk me," she warned, laughter brimming in her voice.

Stuart relished the feel of her as she clung to him. Sexy, sensual and seductive, he thought as he waded into deeper water and she wrapped her legs around his waist to stay afloat. He bobbed up and down in the water.

"I can be bribed into behaving myself," he told her. When her eyebrow raised, he went on, "You know, like at the office. I give my young patients their choice from the 'goodie box' if they don't bite my fingers."

She threaded her fingers into his hair. If he was going to dunk her, she wasn't going under by herself!

"What kind of bribe do you want?"

"A kiss ought to suffice."

"Hmmm." She pretended to give his suggestion serious consideration. Inspired by a trickle of water running down the side of his neck, she dipped her head until her mouth was against a sensitive spot below his chin. She licked the droplet from his skin. "Do I get to bite you first?"

"Wait a second." He chuckled, lowering her deeper into the water. "I'm the one who's being bribed to be good."

She nipped his skin with her teeth, teasing his flesh with her tongue. His hands clamped, pulling her legs from around him. She laced her fingers together behind his head. She felt his throat vibrate and heard his chuckle.

"Lady, you're being very, very wicked."

"And you love it," she chortled gleefully.

His feet were firmly planted on the bottom, her toes dangled against his shins. When she felt herself falling backward, she also felt his lips covering hers.

Underwater kissing was a heady experience for Elaine. Magically, the need for life-sustaining air placed second to the need to deepen the kiss. His breath fed her lungs. The sweet rasping of his velvet tongue across hers fed her secret love.

"God, that was great!" Stuart enthused when their faces broke the surface. His hands pressed her against him. "Wanna do it again?"

Much later, curled up against him on the sofa in her apartment, Elaine whispered her answer. "Again and again and again. Improving on perfection takes practice."

"You should have seen the look on Annette's face when I leaned into the car to kiss you." Stuart smoothed Elaine's hair back from her face. His lips feathered her brow. "I have a distinct feeling cupid doesn't like having her plans changed."

"Or inviting people to dinner who come and go from her house as though it were a revolving door. We really should have stayed longer."

Dropping a kiss on her upturned nose, he asked, "Is that what you wanted to do?"

"Hmmm."

"Don't hmmm a hmmmer. Give me a straight yes or no."

Elaine looked him straight in the eye. "Yes or no."

"Do you know what North Carolinians mean when they call somebody bodacious?"

"Yeah. It's probably your middle name," she replied dryly. She make a tsking noise, as though she'd diagnosed a major defect in his character. "Luring me into the forest, ravaging my body, attempting to drown both of us, then dragging me off to my lair with a charred chicken bone in my mouth." She grinned impudently. "That's bodacious!"

"When we're old and gray, rocking in your rocking chair, I suppose that bit of fiction is what you're going to tell our . . . everybody," he improvised, afraid she'd caught his blunder.

Elaine reached up and lightly patted his flushed cheek. "Grandchildren? No, don't be embarrassed. I don't expect you to walk on eggshells going delete-delete when the word grandchildren, child or baby enters the conversation." She absolved him of his guilt feelings by planting a quick kiss on his lips. "We'd have a hell of a time discussing my work, wouldn't we?"

"Be serious."

"No, thanks," she said with a deadpan expression. "I'd rather be a bodacious mermaid."

He hauled her into his lap, chuckling. His hand skittered down the length of her legs. "Could I convince you to shed your tail and just be a bodacious midwife?''

"Hmmm." She wiggled against him, then fiddled with the button on his pullover shirt. "Could I convince you to take off your shirt?''

Without answering, he snuggled her against his chest, stood and strode toward her bedroom. "Pine needles almost wrecked my knees, sweetheart. Your hardwood floor would have me lying in the dentist's chair with my patients standing over me," he explained. "Besides, I want to make love with you in bed . . . like lovers.''

Elaine could hear the steady beat of his heart beneath her ear. He was everything a woman could want in a lover: affectionate and passionate, witty and charming, but most of all, understanding. She'd never thought she'd be lucky enough to find all those traits in one man.

She sent a silent prayer heavenward. I won't ask for a child, but please, please let him learn to love me.

Dawn hadn't yet arrived when Elaine heard the old-fashioned coiled bedsprings squeaking as Stuart's weight shifted to his side of the bed. He rose silently, gathered his clothes and crossed to the bathroom. She opened her mouth to encourage him to stay just a while longer but closed it before speaking.

Last night he'd needed her. This morning he needed to get dressed, drive to Roanoke Rapids and go to his office. In a few hours she'd be worrying and fussing over her patients and he'd be doing the same.

Oh, for the life of the idle rich, she mused, imagining what it would be like to spend two or three months lazing around in bed. Her conscience promptly prodded her back to reality. She had responsibilities. Who'd care for her patients? She had classes to teach, patients to supervise, babies to deliver. Deep inside, she realized that without their work, both of them would be completely bored within forty-eight hours.

They both needed to be needed.

She pushed aside the bedclothes, stood and stretched. Picking up her silk robe from the chair by the bed, she slipped her arms inside the sleeves and belted it around her trim waist. She went toward the sound of water splashing into the sink.

Bare to the waist, Stuart was hunched in front of the mirror, shaving. He lightly pushed his nose to one side to get the bothersome whiskers above his upper lip. Seeing her reflection in the mirror behind his, he said, "Good morning, sweetheart. I hope you don't mind me borrowing your razor."

"Be my guest," she answered, pleased that he'd made himself at home.

She lingered in the doorway, avidly watching the morning male ritual. The dark stubble he'd acquired during the night was covered with shaving cream. As though the razor were a magic wand, he delicately raked it down his lean face, making his beard disappear. His mouth twisted on one side as he shaved his lower jaw. He rinsed the blade, then followed the same ritual on the other side, his mouth twisting in the opposite direction.

He grinned. Elaine's mouth had echoed the movements of his mouth. "I'll bet a quarter that's something your patients can't do," he joked good-naturedly.

"You'd lose," she replied loftily as she pivoted on one foot and went back into the bedroom. Let him sort that one out, she mused, smiling.

She heard the towel snap without touching her backside. His arms wrapped around her from behind. He dropped one towel, nearly dropping the one knotted at his waist. "Bodaciousness before coffee? You're truly a remarkable woman."

"I could say the same for you," she replied glibly.

"Beautiful, too. All sleepy eyed, with your hair mussed and your face scrubbed clean."

Automatically her hand raised to her face. "You beat me to the bathroom. My face is red from your naughty remarks and from spending the night with a man whose five o'clock shadow has the texture of sandpaper."

"Should I apologize?" His expression was composed, but his eyes danced with wicked delight.

"Do and you'll be standing on Main Street without a towel." She slid her hand languorously down his chest to the towel's knot.

He chuckled, and his eyes dared her to do her worst. He wouldn't have minded if she unlooped his makeshift loincloth. There was something extremely sexy about a woman wearing a shoulder-to-ankle robe with nothing underneath it. The laughter faded from his eyes, leaving them dark, smoldering embers.

"Before coffee?" she murmured. She stood on tip-toe to meet his silent challenge.

With one flick of his wrist, he opened her robe and removed the towel. "Before, during and after."

"Bragging?"

"Begging," he corrected, inching forward and moving her backward.

Her knees touched the edge of the mattress. As agile as he'd been, she twitched her shoulders. Her robe slid to the carpet.

There was no leisurely exploration. Their passion was as full-blown as a late-blooming summer rose.

Afterward they lay entwined, ignoring the sun as it slowly climbed over the two-story building across the street. Both of them dreaded being the one to end the cozy moment.

Stuart picked up her hand and read the face of her wristwatch. "I could cancel my appointments for today."

"I can't. Claire is supposed to come in early to make calls reminding my patients about the class this afternoon. Knowing her, she'd be up here with chicken soup if I faked being ill."

"Chicken soup is my favorite," he teased, imagining the astonished look on Claire's face when she opened the door and found Elaine cuddled up against him. He settled deeper under the blanket. "Have her bring two bowls."

"Annette is my first appointment." She nudged him in the ribs and gave him a sexy wink. "What would you like *her* to bring?"

Stuart shot out of the bed and grabbed his shorts. Hopping from one foot to the other, he shoved his legs into them. "My little sister knows better, but Annette likes to think of me as the equivalent of a male virgin. I'd hate to shock her into delivering prematurely."

Elaine smothered her giggles by pulling his pillow over her head. Annette had often commented on Stuart's success with women. She surfaced for air, saying, "She's a grown woman. Don't you think she knows what goes on between a man and a woman? She's pregnant!"

"She's married!" came from inside his cotton shirt. His head popped through the opening. There was a big smile plastered on his face. Not giving her a chance to react, he bent over Elaine and placed a hearty kiss on her parted lips. "That's something we're going to have to talk about tonight."

Chapter Eight

You two looked as cozy as two bugs in a rug," Annette said, cutting straight to the heart of the matter.

"Good morning to you, too." Elaine pointed to the chart on the table. "Weight, then blood pressure."

"Acceptable and rising," Annette replied concisely, but followed the direction of Elaine's finger. "He's my brother, my only brother. I'm entitled to be curious. God knows he still sticks his big nose in my affairs."

Unable to resist the temptation to tease her, Elaine said, "A pregnant woman, madly in love with her husband, having an affair?"

"Business affairs," Annette corrected, her curiosity momentarily diminished by Elaine's mentioning her pet peeve. "Stuart is constantly interfering in Johnny's work. Mine, too."

"How?" Elaine followed Annette to the upright scale. She moved the weights and found the woman had gained two pounds. Not too bad, considering that the picnic tables had been laden with goodies that were high in calories and low in protein. "Watch it for the rest of the week," she advised.

Nodding, Annette strolled toward the table where the blood pressure kit was kept. "Stuart wants the two of us to distribute our wares through the retail shops in Raleigh and Charlotte."

"That's bad?"

"Money-wise it would be smart, but it means we'd be forced to meet deadlines." Annette nimbly wrapped her upper arm with the steel-gray pad and closed the Velcro straps. She draped the stethoscope around her neck. "Stuart has some peculiar ideas about creative juices. He can't accept the fact that just the thought of designing an afghan and pacing my knitting needles with the second hand on a clock makes me ulcer-prone."

Elaine had developed a keen respect for the independent life-styles of most of the area's residents, Johnny and Annette included. Craftsmen, like farmers, weren't known for having fat bank accounts, but they were rewarded with intangibles. How many pennies was a sunrise worth? The aroma of freshly picked vegetables seasoned with home-grown herbs simmering on the stove wasn't worth two cents at the bank. Offhand, she could think of several things a banker wouldn't record on the credit side of the ledger. The delicate texture of a dogwood blossom. The expression of profound joy on a pregnant woman's face when she feels her baby move for the first time. The sound of a newborn's first gasp for breath.

The quality of their lives was rich, but financially they lived close to the poverty line.

Annette pumped the rubber bulb in her hand. Her eyes were glued to the gauge as she said, "Stuart thinks the real reason I chose to come to you was because we weren't covered by medical insurance. I told you that he threw a fit when I refused to let him pick up the tab for hospital care."

Satisfied that Annette's blood pressure reading was accurate, Elaine handed her the clipboard with her monthly progress chart attached. "We'll have to reeducate him, won't we?"

Annette grimaced comically. "I'd have better luck making peach preserves from cucumbers. I'll have to admit, though, he hasn't hassled us since he visited your clinic."

A warm, rosy glow of pleasure tinged Elaine's cheeks. "Just goes to prove that you can teach an old dog new tricks, huh?"

Annette's hearty chuckle reminded her of Stuart's when he was planning a mischievous prank. His sister didn't disappoint Elaine. She patted her thigh and whistled as though she were calling a four-legged animal.

"You'd be flabbergasted if he came skittering down the steps," Elaine said dryly, recalling what Stuart had said regarding Annette's "halo" impression of him.

"Wrong. That's strictly his impression of what *I'd* think." She swung the earpieces of the stethoscope in a wide arc. Her voice dripped with false innocence as she inquired, "I wonder who told you I'd be flabbergasted?"

Elaine shrugged her shoulders as though she didn't have the faintest idea what Annette was talking about. She wasn't going to tattle on Stuart. If he'd wanted his sister to know where he'd spent the night, he wouldn't have bolted from her bed. She'd have to watch her tongue, or Annette wasn't going to have any difficulty putting two and two together and coming up with the right answers.

She could have hugged Claire when she drew Annette's attention by unintentionally slamming the storage room door. Claire stepped into the open area carrying an armful of booklets of the Lamaze technique.

"Hi, Annette," Claire said, handing Annette a booklet.

Annette took the brochure, gazing at Claire thoughtfully. "Something is missing," she said with a grin. Then it occurred to her. "Where's your gum?"

"Elaine says I chew gum like the Rice Krispies kids—Snap, Crackle and Pop." Annette giggled; Elaine rolled her eyes toward the ceiling at the indiscreet revelation. Claire grinned, neatly stacking the remainder of the booklets on a table. "Gotta take the good with the bad."

"We were just discussing the good, the bad and the ugly," Annette said, knowing Claire would jump at the chance to find out what was going on between Elaine and Stuart.

"Midwives, o.b.'s and stretch marks?" Claire responded gamely.

"Uh-uh," Annette countered. "Mothers, brothers and straitlaced yuppies."

Elaine suppressed a grin at the verbal sparring and stepped toward the safety of her office. "I have some work to do in the privacy of my office. I'm certain you two clever ladies will excuse me."

"Wrong!" Claire and Annette chorused after exchanging a conspiratorial glance.

Elaine groaned aloud, certain they wouldn't have any qualms about stepping on her toes to keep her from departing. She shifted her weight, thrusting one hip forward aggressively. Mimicking the voice of one of the villains on Claire's soap opera, she waved a fist, threatening, "You're both cruisin' for a bruisin'."

"She wouldn't try to intimidate us unless she had something to hide," Annette whispered to her cohort.

Elaine saw them exchange another predatory glance before they chimed, "Right!" in unison.

"Confessions obtained under duress are invalid," Elaine warned. Her toe tapped on the hardwood floor. "I'll lie."

"She doesn't know how to lie," Claire confided out of the side of her mouth. "She may walk a wide circle around the truth to be evasive, but she won't lie."

"Stop muttering to each other as though I can't hear you."

"We're getting to her," Annette crowed, sidling up to Elaine and putting her arm across her shoulders. Over her shoulder she whispered, "She's gonna spill the beans."

Elaine shook her shoulders to free herself, then folded her arms across her chest. "I watch television, too. You aren't going to trap me into confessing anything with a good-cop-bad-cop method of interrogation. Fun's fun, but playtime is over."

Whirling around, Elaine retreated, briskly striding to her glass-enclosed cubicle. By the time she plopped into her desk chair, Annette and Claire were huddled together, arguing quietly. Seconds later, they fired a double round of dirty looks in her direction. She knew they'd grudgingly admitted defeat when Claire pecked the Lamaze training booklet with her finger and Annette opened it.

In preparation for her afternoon class, Elaine opened her filing cabinet and removed a notebook containing her lecture notes. She flipped past the section on exercise, eating and the mechanics of birth, also skipping the lessons on back rubs and breathing techniques. They'd review those techniques, but today she wanted to concentrate on emotional stages during delivery: self-doubts and suggestibility. The mother-to-be had to be reassured that wondering why-didn't-I-go-to-a-hospital-where-they-knock-me-out often occurred before the pushing stage started. Praise from their husbands was crucial at this point.

Her mind wandered from the printed material to Stuart's parting remark. "She's married. We'll have to talk about that tonight."

What a cliff-hanger, she mused, grinning. She'd gotten to know him well enough not to assume he wanted to discuss his sister's marriage. His contemplating marriage would have Annette oiling up the shotgun if Elaine confided in her. The last thing she wanted was to have Annette pushing at the wrong time.

Marriage, she thought silently, uncertain whether she wanted to be swept into another commitment. Any divorcée with a lick of common sense was cautious the second time around. Hundreds of clichés were appropriate here, and they all warned against acting impetuously.

Elaine ran her tongue over her bottom lip.

Conversely, the thought of having someone to confide in, to wake up with and find sharing her pillow was appealing. Subliminally she heard Bob York's rendition of "Friends and Lovers." The mellow tones of his saxophone reached out to her. There were no lyrics, but his music evoked feelings of longing.

Seduced by the memory of the haunting melody, Elaine leaned back in her chair. She closed her eyes. Instantly an image of Stuart filled the black void.

Minutes later, she'd fallen asleep without resolving her dilemma or making a decision.

"...touch her. Tell your wife she's doing just great. Let her know that shortly she'll be holding a baby in her arms."

Elaine heard a rude snort coming from Margery's and Tom's direction. She ignored three previous snortlike sounds he'd made. Each one had become progressively louder, more defiant, more obnoxious.

She should have been aware of his intentions when he'd arrived late, walking in as though he were the local banker and owned a bigger share of the building than she did. He'd sprawled in his chair, pulled his straw hat low on his forehead and twirled his sunglasses.

Familiar with Tom's benign neglect of his wife, she fully understood his attempt to draw everyone's attention in his direction. He'd accomplished his goal. Other members in the small group were shuffling their feet uncomfortably, darting glances at him.

Tom Clements had spoiled her effectiveness. She could tolerate his being discourteous to her, but she'd be damned if the others had to put up with his crude behavior.

Turning to face him directly, she asked sweetly, "Are you in need of a tissue?"

"Naw," he drawled. "I could use a cold beer though. My throat is a mite dry from listenin' to all this here woman's talk."

Margery's face blanched. Her makeup stood out as though a heavy-handed clown had applied it. Elaine could tell she wanted to crawl under her chair and die of humiliation.

"Refreshments will be served shortly," Elaine replied. The firm control she held on her temper was slipping. "Now as I was saying—"

"Artificially sweetened Kool-Aid 'n' cookies ain't what I'd call refreshin'," Tom said. "Why don't you git somethin' a man can drink?"

Elaine forced herself to smile, silently ordering her hand not to clench.

"We're listening to you, Elaine," Johnny said, his voice bristling.

"I'm not," Tom blustered, sliding his sunglasses down his nose and faking a loud snore.

Johnny moved to the edge of the sofa's cushion and was close to rising when Elaine raised her hand to stop him. She didn't need a man to fight her battles; she had the battle scars to prove it.

"Would you all mind skimming the booklet while Tom and I step into the office for a few minutes?" she asked. Inbred poise allowed her to rise gracefully and cross the width of the room without so much as a backward glance to make certain Tom was following her.

Unknown to the others, she was shaking with fury on the inside. How she'd love to tell him what she thought of him as a husband and father. Tom had more in common with his precious damned fish than he did with the human species. Elaine ardently wished she could throw Tom back into the lake. Margery had caught him, but he definitely wasn't a keeper.

"Be seated, please," she said, seating herself behind her desk. "I'll get straight to the point, Tom. It was your idea for Margery to come to the Mother's Clinic, and yet you balk at attending the meetings or you make snide remarks on the rare occasions when you do bless us with your presence. What's the problem?"

Tom hunched toward her, lazily circling the brim of his straw hat in his hands. "You. First you git us to sign up by tellin' us havin' a kid at home is just a normal everyday happenin'. Now you're tryin' to make a big deal out of it."

"How?"

"Come on, missy," he drawled. "You preach 'bout doin' things natural. In my book, givin' a woman a back rub is unnatural. She's supposed to be rubbin' my back. I'm the one out there sweatin' and toilin', earnin' enough money to keep a roof over her head and clothes on her back. That's another thing." He pointed his tobacco-stained index finger squarely between her eyes. "I got my pride. I may be poor, but I ain't no charity case. I don't want my woman wearin' somebody's castoffs. Don't send any more second-hand clothes out to my farm."

Keeping silent while he berated her was easy. Elaine had her teeth clenched tighter than a person who'd had his jaws wired together. She tenaciously clung to the remnants of her temper as she spoke on Margery's behalf.

"Your wife wants to have the baby at home. She wants you with her, helping her."

"Horsefeathers! Do you know what I think? She wants to get even with me for goin' fishin'. It's her big chance to make me listen to her hollerin' without me yellin' back at her."

His twisted reasoning brought Elaine to her feet. Hands bracing her rigid arms, she used his own barn-yard terminology against him. "Horsefeathers is right! Why don't you take off those sunglasses of yours, look around and see what's going on? A man couldn't ask for a better wife or two nicer kids."

"That's 'cause I know how to keep my womenfolk straight. No thanks to you and your highfalutin' ideas."

"Let me get this right. You don't approve of me or the Mother's Clinic or the influence I have on your wife."

Tom grinned. "You're smarter than I thought. I didn't have to draw you a cartoon picture or nuthin'."

Turning, Elaine yanked the filing cabinet drawer open and pulled out Margery's file. She could waste her breath trying to change his attitude for his wife's sake, but in the long run she knew it was Margery who would suffer. If Margery couldn't count on his assisting her now, he'd be a total failure when she truly needed him.

Elaine tossed the file across the desk. "Take this with you when you leave," she commanded quietly.

"What?" Stunned, he reared back in his seat. "You can't kick me out of here."

"You heard me. Take your hat and your sunglasses and your crude noises and get out."

Puffed up like a toad, Tom angrily heaved himself to his feet. "No woman talks to Tom Clements like he's a junkyard dog. I'm the man who pays the bills. You oughta show me respect."

"Respect, like my fee, is earned. *O-U-T.*"

Tom scooped up the file in his beefy hand. Crossing to the door, he raised his voice for everyone to hear. "I'm takin' Margery to a real doctor. A man knows better than to put crazy notions in a woman's head. He won't talk ugly to her husband, neither."

Looking through the glass panel separating the two rooms, Elaine saw the stricken expression on Margery's face. For an instant Elaine thought she saw a mutinous glitter in Margery's eyes, but she must have been mistaken. Tom snapped his fingers in his wife's direction. Loyalty prevailed. Margery traipsed meekly after him through the outside door.

While the other patients whispered quietly among themselves, Elaine considered what had happened. Could she have avoided an open confrontation? Tom had deliberately provoked her, but there must have been some way of salvaging the situation without resorting to ordering him off the premises.

Wait a minute, she thought, stopping her search for viable options. She was definitely in favor of natural childbirth, but she was open-minded enough to realize it wasn't the only method of delivering a baby or, in all cases, the safest.

Her first concern had to be for the mother and the unborn child. Specifically, what was best for Margery. She'd had minor complications throughout the months she'd been coming to the Mother's Clinic. Considering her home environment, who wouldn't? Tom had made his decision to bring his wife to the clinic using two criteria: money and convenience.

Elaine could have worked around that problem. The services she rendered were far more extensive than those of most of the nearby obstetricians. She had faith that most of her patients appreciated the lower cost. Tom firmly believed she was some sort of bargain-basement doctor. He didn't pay as much, therefore the quality must be inferior.

Although she'd paid special attention to Margery's progress, Tom hadn't changed his opinion.

So what should she have done? Charged him more? Fined him each time he missed a class? Made him pay a penalty for neglecting his wife?

Elaine shook her head. Tom complicated Margery's pregnancy. Physically she was well within the normal range, but emotionally she was in the high-risk category. If anything, Elaine thought, she should have sent Margery to a doctor sooner.

Still, she couldn't help feeling as though she'd failed Margery. Her chin raised a fraction of an inch. A professional couldn't let pride get in the way of sound judgment.

Later, she promised herself, she'd ask Stuart what he would have done under similar circumstances. The thought of sharing her problems with him boosted her spirits. Regardless of what warped story Tom spread around the community, she had faith that Stuart would back her.

Stuart mounted the fire escape behind the Mother's Clinic two steps at a time. Disheveled and panting, he crossed the metal landing outside Elaine's bedroom. She wasn't in the clinic. A Closed sign hung on the front door, the interior was pitch-black. He'd jogged along the sidewalk searching for a staircase leading to the upper floor. There were none that led to her apartment, only a stairwell allowing access to the second floor of the building next door. From the street, he couldn't see any lights shining from the windows of Elaine's apartment.

The thought of Elaine purposely locking him out had him seriously considering breaking and entering.

He'd left once before thinking everything between them was fine. Surely after last night she couldn't have changed her mind again, he thought. Anxiety and exertion had his heart hammering in his chest.

He shaded his face to block the sun's rays and peered into the interior. Black shades had been lowered. The window was mirrorlike. His own distraught image bounced back at him. Frustrated, he pounded his knuckles against the sheet of glass.

Inside, Elaine groggily uncurled from her sleeping position. Automatically she glanced at the clock and reached for her beeper at the same time. Six o'clock. Morning or night? she wondered, disoriented.

She remembered closing the clinic shortly after Tom had stormed out and the others had left. Exhausted from lack of sleep and emotional fatigue, she'd wearily climbed the steps leading from the kitchen downstairs to her apartment kitchen. She'd intended to straighten up her apartment and make the bed before Stuart arrived, but the rumpled sheets and blankets had been too inviting to resist. She'd pulled down the blackout shade and pitched face first onto the pillow Stuart had used. A hint of his fragrance had lingered. Smiling, she'd wrapped her arms around it and fallen sound asleep.

"Elaine! Open the window or I'll take off my shoe and break the damned thing!"

Leaping off the bed, she scurried across the room and yanked up on the blackout shade. Stuart had one hand on the glass and the other on the heel of his shoe. For some reason unknown to Elaine, he was flaming mad. She could faintly hear the mild expletives he muttered to himself.

She couldn't open the window. He hadn't noticed the blind spinning, either. She placed her hand on the opposite side of the glass, tapping her fingers on his heartline.

His scowl turned into a radiant smile when he felt her tap. He dropped his shoe, straightened and called, "Let me in?"

The wooden window frame was sealed with several layers of paint. Obviously he doesn't know a thing about restored buildings, she thought, shaking her head and pointing her finger downward. Understanding her gesture, Stuart picked up his shoe and retreated down the fire escape.

In a flash she was unlocking the door, welcoming him with a wide smile and open arms. One shoe off and one shoe on, Stuart crossed the threshold and crushed her against his chest.

"Hi," she murmured against his lips, feeling giddy.

"Hi, yourself." He dropped his shoe and kicked the door shut with his foot. His lips greedily covered hers for one short, hard kiss. That was all he could allow himself, otherwise... His honorable intentions of discussing marriage before claiming her began to fade as her tongue slipped inside his mouth.

Elaine closed her eyes when she felt him sip at her tongue, stroking the underside with the tip of his, then swirling it until she was dizzy with frustration. She laughed breathlessly against his lips, then let her head loll back against his forearm.

He peppered kisses over her face as he asked, "How was your day?"

"Awful."

"Mine, too."

"Better now, though," she sighed. "Much better."

Music to my ears, he thought. "Miss me?"

"Terribly."

"Good. Between patients I must have picked up the phone a dozen times." Indecisiveness didn't sit well with him. At lunch he'd found himself plucking petals off a daisy from the centerpiece. She loves me; she loves me not. I love her; she loves me. Fortunately, the petals had landed in his salad. Rather than explain his sappy behavior to the man seated across from him, he'd tossed the stem aside, poured Italian dressing over the petals and eaten them.

Right then and there, he'd vowed to get a definite answer from Elaine. He'd eaten his last flower salad.

"You didn't call me. Why?"

"Three reasons. One—historically I've had lousy luck reaching you by phone." He paused, waiting for her to relieve the fear that had prevented him from picking up the receiver and dialing her number—fear of rejection.

"You know I'd have talked to you unless I was busy with one of my patients."

He'd dared to hope, but he hadn't known for certain. His hand roamed over her hips, rocking her against his thighs. The proof of his desire coincided with the achy sensation slowly building in the pit of her stomach.

"You thought I'd call you, didn't you?" Elaine asked.

Chuckling, Stuart shook his head. "No. I've learned better than to expect the quarry to do an about-face and start chasing the hunter. But that does bring me to the second reason. I know how you feel about doctors interfering with the natural chain of events. Which brings me to the third reason."

"Whoa, Dr. Cimarron, back up." She lightly put her fingers over his mouth to stop his flow of words. "Aren't you overgeneralizing a mite? Professionally, I'll admit to verbalizing strong objections to having the normal stages of a woman's delivery interfered with." Her fingers dropped to his loosened necktie and untied it completely. "You, my dear doctor, are a dentist, not an obstetrician."

"True, but I was interfering when I coerced Annette into introducing me to her midwife."

She tugged on one end of his silk tie. The delicious sound of silk sliding over cotton brought a more recent memory to mind: a cotton towel and a silk robe. Were they still lying on top of each other on the carpet? Distracted by the image crowding her thoughts, she merely nodded to confirm that she'd heard what Stuart had said.

Watching her closely, he noticed the dark pupils of her eyes widening until the blue-green irises thinned to a narrow band. He'd come to know what was going on behind those lovely eyes of hers. While she slowly, methodically undressed him, her thoughts winged upstairs. His stomach muscles quivered with the knowledge that she wanted him as much as he needed her.

"Marriage," he blurted out, startling her and instantly regaining her attention.

Her head snapped up, her reverie abruptly ending. "Marriage?"

"My third reason for not calling you." He chuckled as her eyes clouded with confusion. She was wondering if she'd missed something while she'd been daydreaming. "I told you we'd talk about marriage tonight. I didn't want to discuss it on the phone."

She'd been caught off guard, and only one word had penetrated her wayward thoughts. Her mouth dry, she repeated, "Marriage," as though it were a particularly difficult tongue twister.

His innate male hunting instincts cautioned him against closing in on his quarry too quickly, but he didn't listen to the inner warning. "I placed a call to city hall. There's a three-day waiting period in North Carolina."

The corners of her mouth turned down. Three days? She'd dated Joe for eighteen months before she'd accepted his proposal. Then they'd waited another six months before they'd married. It had taken over a year for her to decide to start divorce proceedings. Three days was hardly longer than the blink of an eye in comparison.

And yet the overwhelming desire to grab him, hang on tightly and shout, "Yes, yes, yes," had her inching away from him until his hands could scarcely reach her. Once she'd put a little distance between them, she knew she'd be able to think clearly.

She ran her hands nervously down the side seams of her slacks. "What about children?"

"One step at a time," he replied, closing the gap between them. "Does the thought of marriage make your hands tremble and your heart race?"

"No." Her head bobbed up and down, then shook from side to side, revealing her state of confusion. "I mean, yes."

Oh, hell, what did she mean? Why hadn't he waited until later to ask? How much later? Would where or when make any difference?

Stuart couldn't stop the slow grin from lifting his lips at the thought of having a steady diet of daisy salads. Reaching forward, he weaved his fingers through her hair and brought her head back to his chest. "Sweetheart, I'd like nothing better than to throw you over my shoulder and take you to the nearest preacher, but I can wait if you can answer one question."

"I'll try," she promised.

He paused, uncertain. "Do you love me?"

She arched her eyebrows and looked at him as though he were the one who'd lost his reasoning faculties. "Is a forty-pound robin fat if he ain't long?"

"Yes?" His eyes were twinkling, even though he'd restrained himself from laughing aloud at her nonsensical quip.

"I... love... you." She enunciated each word slowly, clearly, so there would be no doubts in his mind on that score. She linked her hand with his and led him toward the steps. "You could return the compliment."

"You haven't seen any tall forty-pound robins in this neck of the woods, have you?"

Tossing her head back, she laughed, dancing up the steps ahead of him. "I'm not the only one around here who's bodacious."

"You aren't the only one around here in love, either."

An hour later, Stuart was elbow-deep in soapsuds, washing dishes while Elaine cleared off the table. Spaghetti had never tasted so good. Silently he admitted that she could have served him arsenic and he wouldn't have objected as long as she'd liberally sprinkled kisses on him while she'd served it.

"Did I tell you that Annette and Claire tried to pry information out of me first thing this morning?"

"Great way to start your day, huh?"

"Yeah. Especially when I'm bleary-eyed from lack of sleep." She scraped the remains of the meat sauce into a bowl, picked up the sharp knife she'd used to slice the French bread and headed toward the bedroom.

Stuart tracked her with his eyes, seldom letting her out of his sight. Strange, he mused, cocking his head to one side in bewilderment. Leftovers at his house were usually tossed into the garbage disposal or put in the refrigerator. Why would she take the spaghetti sauce into the bedroom? Did she plan to eat it later? Without noodles? With a knife? He dried his hands on a dishtowel and followed her.

Elaine had placed the sauce on the nightstand and moved a chair next to the window. She heard a floorboard squeak behind her just as she stepped on the chair.

"Mind if I ask what the hell you're doing?"

"Feeding Clunker."

He nodded as though her reply made perfectly good sense. She'd brought spaghetti sauce into the bedroom to feed her car. Yeah, why not? Pretty soon he'd be saying yes and shaking his head, too. Or was it saying no and nodding his head? Whatever, it had to take practice.

"I could use some help," she hinted, holding the knife out to him.

Couldn't we all, he thought, uncertain of how she expected him to help. Hell, he'd never fed his Mercedes. He just filled it up with gas like other normal folks.

"What would you like me to do?"

"Get the window open."

"With the knife." He took the knife and looked at the unlocked window. Why didn't she just lift it up? Surely she didn't want him to stand on the chair, heave the knife through the window and pitch the spaghetti down on her car.

"Well?" She saw his lips twitch. His eyes were sparkling with mirth. What was funny about cutting through three coats of paint to get the window open? "It's stuck."

"So am I. I feel like I've opened a package that contains a million parts with the directions written in braille. Just what exactly are you trying to accomplish?"

"I'm going to feed the cat the leftovers from dinner."

"A clunker is a cat?"

"Of course."

He shrugged. "I thought a clunker was a car."

Now Elaine was getting confused. She shot him a peculiar look. "I put gas in my car. Wouldn't spaghetti sauce muck up the engine?"

"I was just wondering the same thing about feeding it to the cat."

"Clunker eats anything that doesn't bite first. Now, about the window..."

"Yeah." When he caught himself shaking his head, he burst out laughing. "Throw it through the window, right?"

"Are you daft?" Elaine remembered his telling her that her hot-and-cold treatment was driving him crazy. Why was he laughing like a maniac? Was he giving her a firsthand demonstration? "Is this a private joke, or can anybody join in?"

"I think I'd better put the knife down," he said between bouts of laughter. He dropped the knife on the windowsill. "I don't trust myself with a sharp instrument."

Elaine was sure he was a bit touched in the head when he grabbed her around the waist and tumbled her into the bed. "Stuart!"

He forgot what he'd found so damned funny when she rolled him onto his back and straddled him. Her hands held his wrists beside his head. Fear of losing his sanity increased tenfold when she settled on top of him. "I'm crazy about you, lady."

"You're just plain old crazy," she huffed.

"I'll explain later, but right now..." With a flick of his wrist, he freed one hand and hauled her down until her mouth touched his.

All thoughts of the cat and the dishes and the rotten day she'd had at work were scorched from her memory as flames burst into wildfire inside her.

She could feel his hands running down her back in a frenzied motion. Feverishly she grappled with the buttons on her blouse. Either the buttons had grown while she hadn't been watching or the holes had shrunk. She couldn't master the simple task of undressing herself.

"Let me," Stuart said, coaxing her fingers out of the way. He was as inept as she'd been, but he was stronger. With one swift jerk, buttons popped and her blouse opened. He dispensed with the remainder of their clothes with the same abandoned recklessness.

Her mouth moved on his skin. She nipped his shoulder, heat and salt and his earthy scent combined. Her lips, teeth and tongue teased and tormented until his fingers tunneled into her hair, guiding her mouth to his. Elaine shuddered. His brash kiss—not soft, not tender—fanned the flames.

She was astride him in a position that allowed her dominance, and yet she conformed to the subtle command of his hands as they linked her hips to his. Her fingers curled into the dark mat of hair as she raised herself up on her knees. Beneath her hands she felt a low groan building in his chest. It rumbled from between his lips, an admission of his fierce need. She descended until they were inseparably bonded together. An involuntary muscle contracted, capturing him, holding him deep within her.

Pleasure jolted through her. Her hips rotated, his hips lifted, fell, then drove higher, filling her with his urgency. Tiny pulsing tremors constricted her insides, creating friction, permitting him to recede when she chose, refusing when she hadn't had enough of him. Raw, primitive instincts unleashed her from civilized inhibitions. Mindlessly she took what she wanted, unaware that in the taking she was driving him beyond the boundaries of ecstasy that he'd previously known—even with her.

He was barely lucid, the blood pounding in his ears and deafening him to his own garbled cries. Whatever glitches there were in their verbal communication, they were clarified as their bodies spoke passionately in a primeval language.

She held Stuart; he held her. Her blue eyes, flecked with yellow, shone a brilliant emerald blue; his brown eyes, darkened by desire, blazed like polished onyx. As they both peaked, an invisible bond of love was forged between them.

Elaine rolled over, then automatically turned onto her back and raised her knees to her chest. What had the specialist said? To increase the possibility of the sperm fertilizing the egg, elevate your hips. Her eyes blinked hard. Lowering her legs, she realized that one of the joys of making love with Stuart was not having to assume such an unnatural position. No charts, no thermometers, no regimentation, she thought, smiling. Spontaneous lovemaking was deliciously satisfying.

Stuart turned onto his side. "You look like a cat who just polished off a bowl of cream."

"Spaghetti sauce... Which reminds me, we didn't get the window open. When I don't take leftovers downstairs, Clunker gets disgruntled. She clunks up the stairs and meows outside the window until I feed her."

"Now your taking leftovers into the bedroom is beginning to make sense." The love-swollen lips he'd so thoroughly kissed enticed him. Sweet, he thought, moving his lips tenderly back and forth over hers. He'd never get enough of her. He felt her lips curve and heard Clunker's meow at the same time. "Guess I'd better get the window open to save you a trip downstairs, hmmm?"

She nodded. "Clunker's manners are deplorable. She'll cause a terrible racket if she's ignored."

"I think I'm going to love that cat." He flung his legs off the bed, chuckled when he saw the condition of his clothing and strode into the bathroom. "From here on out, Clunker and I are going to have something in common."

Elaine followed his line of thinking. "You're going to howl outside my window if you're ignored?"

"Exactly." After he'd cleaned up, he ran water over a washcloth and took it to Elaine. "Only I won't be raising a ruckus for merely a dinner date."

There was little doubt in her mind why he'd cause a commotion if she ignored him. The feeling was mutual. "I guess I'd better have another key made."

Stuart picked up his slacks. He zipped them but couldn't button them at the waist. The button was missing. Who cares about clothes? he mused with a wide grin. He'd much rather have a key.

Chapter Nine

My place or yours?"

Not a difficult question, Elaine thought as she hung up the phone. Tonight, after a meeting, he'd come to her place. He'd be later than usual, but he'd be there.

During the past six weeks she'd spent as much time at his house as he'd spent at her apartment. When they wanted to take advantage of the entertainment offered in Roanoke Rapids, they'd end up at his house. Conversely, when they planned on going to the lake or enjoying long country walks, he'd spend the night with her.

Clunker must have thought she'd died and gone to stray-cat heaven. Stuart absolutely refused to let the cat shift for herself while Elaine was gone. Remembering how he'd had to chase Clunker to get her into his car the first time Elaine had agreed to stay in

Roanoke Rapids brought a lingering smile to her lips. She was just like the cat. Stuart had chased her until he'd caught her and made her realize she was much better off with him than without him. And—again like Clunker—she'd been changed by his tender, loving care.

They'd spend hours talking, getting to know each other's foibles. She'd admitted to being overly cautious, to thinking too much before acting. Fence-sitting, he'd jokingly called her behavior. He'd agreed that he had a habit of reacting, then reconsidering if he made a bad initial decision. Jumping off the fence before you see where you're going to land, she'd countered. Neither of them had actually contemplated changing, but gradually, in little ways, they had. He'd begun looking at both sides of the picture before dashing off a note, and she'd begun to read his notes without studying every word for hidden meanings.

Seldom did she worry her bottom lip when Stuart was around. His outrageous sense of humor knew no boundaries when it came to making her laugh. Since he'd been taking her to Gaston Lake regularly, her usual pale skin had been transformed by a golden tan. She hadn't realized how much weight she'd lost since her divorce until she'd noticed that her clothes no longer hung loose but fit snugly over her feminine curves. She radiated the good health and happiness that she recommended for her patients.

Elaine flipped her desk calendar backward. She'd met Stuart in June, made love with him for the first time in July, and now, in September...her daydreaming came to an abrupt halt. Out of habit, she still kept an accurate record of her monthly cycle by placing a red check on the page.

Where were the check marks? Frantic, she hurriedly shuffled back through the pages. There weren't any in July or August! Had she left them out because she'd been unconcerned or because she hadn't had a period? Think, Elaine, she demanded silently as she pulled her lower lip beneath her teeth.

She must have forgotten. Not having to worry about keeping a bedside chart, she must have become lax about keeping track of her monthly cycle. She was usually due in the middle of the month. No notation entered there. She turned a couple more pages as she tried to reconstruct her personal calendar.

That doesn't mean a damned thing, she silently grumbled. Part of her problem when she'd been trying to get pregnant had been her irregularity. She'd missed a whole month once, and it had meant nothing but having her hopes elevated for nothing.

She turned several more pages. Why hadn't she marked anything in August? Usually, if she did miss, the next month made up for it.

Opening the bottom drawer of her desk, she pulled out her checkbook and looked at the calendar on the back page. Her brow knitted together. Nothing was circled except the approximate due dates of her patients.

She refused to jump to the logical conclusion. She couldn't be pregnant. That was nearly impossible. Nearly...but not absolutely, she mused. Other women became pregnant after having a tubal pregnancy. She shook her head, totally perplexed. She couldn't be pregnant. She'd used every scrap of medical advice known to the medical profession, plus a few old midwives' superstitions, to get pregnant when she'd been married to Joe. Wouldn't it be ironic if...

Elaine put her hand over her heart. She felt a fluttering sensation in her chest as her hopes began to blossom. God, wouldn't it be wonderful? Remembering the promise she'd made when she'd prayed for Stuart to love her as much as she loved him, Elaine's grin turned into a scowl.

It was too much to ask. Stuart loved her, that was enough.

Automatically, despite her certainty that she wasn't pregnant, she began mentally reciting the symptoms of being an expectant mother. Her breasts weren't sore, but they were sensitive. She'd attributed their tenderness to Stuart's heavy beard. She hadn't been sick to her stomach when she'd had the tubal pregnancy, either.

Rising to her feet, she began to pace. She did seem to require more sleep lately. A wry grin spread across her face. Sleeping and going to bed weren't synonymous, not with Stuart sharing her bed.

Before she realized where she was going she'd walked out of her office and through the front door and was headed toward the drugstore. There was no point in dithering. Either she was pregnant, which she highly doubted, or she wasn't pregnant, which she didn't dare think about. One way or another, a simple test kit would answer the question.

Thirty minutes later, Elaine walked out of the bathroom in her office. Totally dazed, she sank into her desk chair. She felt like laughing, crying and jumping up and down with joy.

The test indicated that she was pregnant!

"I'm going to have a baby," she murmured. She repeated the fact over and over until she was finally able to believe it. "I'm going to be a mother!"

Hugging herself, she reached for the phone. Stuart! She had to tell him. No, wait, she thought, glancing at her watch. He would have already left for his Lions Club executive board meeting. Where had he told her they were meeting? She couldn't remember. At the time he'd told her, she hadn't thought knowing his exact location was important.

She'd have to wait until tonight to tell him. She could hardly wait to see the expression on his face. He'd be over the moon with happiness.

The one barrier that had prevented her from accepting his proposal had been eliminated. She'd lost one husband because she hadn't been able to have a child; she'd needed time to make certain Stuart loved her even though he'd never be a father. Feeling truly blessed, she whispered, "Stuart's going to be a daddy. I'm going to have his baby!"

She was bursting to tell someone the good news. Who? Claire? Annette? No, that would be wrong. She'd just have to contain herself until Stuart came home.

As she left her office and climbed the stairs to her apartment, she whistled merrily, a lighthearted joy filling her soul.

Tap-dancing her way across the living room, she put Bob York's recording of the song "Tea for Two" on the phonograph. Clunker uncurled from the corner of the sofa, stretched and yawned. Elaine twirled around and picked her up.

Holding the cat like a newborn, Elaine said, "Guess what? I'm going to have a baby."

Clunker blinked, unimpressed. Turning her head toward the kitchen, she sniffed the air delicately.

"You say you're more interested in dinner than my being pregnant?" Elaine heard her purr and felt the animal's vibration in her hand. Beneath her newly acquired thick coat of silky fur, she felt Clunker's pouchy stomach. "Look how fat and lazy you're getting. Stuart spoils you rotten."

At the sound of Stuart's name, Clunker gracefully hopped from Elaine's arms and sashayed to the door. Cocking her head, she mewed sorrowfully.

"He's coming, but he's going to be late. Come on, I'll feed you." Elaine watched Clunker cross to the kitchen. She had gained a suspicious amount of weight. "You aren't eating for five or six, are you?"

Cats can't talk or smile or blush, but Elaine could have sworn Clunker wanted to do all three.

"Hmmm. Guess you need more crunchies then, huh, Clunker?"

As she fixed the cat's dinner, she changed her mind about what she was going to fix for herself. When Stuart had called to remind her that he wouldn't be home for dinner, she'd planned on heating up a frozen pizza. A salad, lean meat and a piece of fruit, she thought, altering the menu. She'd have to watch her diet now that she was eating for two.

"Eating for two," she murmured, saying the thought aloud, cherishing the idea. She glanced down at her flat stomach. She could hardly wait to shop for maternity clothes.

She put Clunker's bowl down on the floor. "Okay, Clunker. No more raiding the local garbage pails. We're both going to watch what we eat."

Clunker twitched her tail, eyed the cat food and sauntered back into the living room.

"Persnickety cat," Elaine muttered, dismissing the cat's haughty meow.

While she prepared dinner, she hummed along with the record and fantasized. Should she meet Stuart at the door and blurt, "We're gonna have a baby!" Or should she dim the lights and share a glass of wine with him before she made the announcement? Or maybe she should bring up the subject of marriage first. This time, knowing he truly loved her, knowing he accepted her for her weaknesses as well as her strengths, she could accept . . . Then she'd tell him—if she could wait that long, which she seriously doubted.

After Elaine had eaten dinner and given Clunker the leftover scraps of meat, she cleaned the kitchen, then went into her bedroom and selected a feminine nightie from her bottom drawer. She'd shower, wash her hair, dab her favorite perfume in strategic spots and wait for him in bed.

His shoes in his hand, Stuart quietly climbed the steps from the Mother's Clinic to Elaine's apartment. It had been one of those days. June had called in sick at the last minute. He'd had to make all the preparations for the patients, answer the phone and schedule new appointments. Without June there to remind him, he'd forgotten about the Lions Club meeting until late afternoon. When he'd wanted to do nothing more than relax in front of the television with Elaine on his lap, he'd had to hash over the qualifications of the men to run for the executive board. The slate they'd selected would be presented at the next general meeting. Just to round out the disastrous day, he'd had a flat tire on the way to Tyler.

He glanced at the illuminated dial of his watch. Ten-thirty, he groaned silently. By now Elaine would probably be sound asleep in front of the television. The thought of carrying her into the bedroom and making slow, leisurely love to her brought a smile to his face.

Opening the door, he listened for any sounds coming from the television, but there were none. The only light came from the bedroom. Clunker greeted him, swishing between his legs, begging for attention. Stuart reached down and scooped the cat into his arms.

"What are you doing in here when Elaine has gone to bed?" he whispered.

Clunker made herself comfortable and purred loudly.

"Did you eat?"

She rubbed her head against his shirt, then burrowed her nose between his bent arm and his rib cage.

"Hmmm." He scratched her ears. If Elaine hadn't fed Clunker, she'd have been making a pitiful sound. "You're getting lazy, old girl. I guess you think I ought to carry you in the bedroom and put you in your basket, huh?"

Admit it, Stuart thought, you enjoy spoiling Clunker as much as you enjoy spoiling Elaine. But in all honesty, he had to admit that Elaine did more of the spoiling than he did. In fact, he'd had to learn not to drop the slightest hint or Elaine would construe it as his heart's wildest desire and do everything she could to fulfill his wish. From cooking extravagant desserts to buying him shirts, she pampered him outrageously.

Stuart settled Clunker in her basket and approached the bed. Lord, she's beautiful, he mused as he began removing his clothes. She slept on her side, facing the empty part of the bed. One hand was tucked under her pillow, the other rested on his pillow. Her face was partially covered by a dark tress of silky hair, but he could see a small smile curving her lips, as though she were having a pleasant dream.

Undressed, he started to awaken her but decided he'd be a selfish lout to disturb her sleep. There was always tomorrow. Usually, when Elaine went to bed early, she awakened early. Many a morning they'd made love before dawn.

Painstakingly he eased her hand aside and slid between the sheets. It was enough for now just knowing they were sharing the same bed.

Stuart had barely closed his eyes when the phone rang. Before he could get out of bed to answer it, Elaine rolled over and picked up the receiver.

"Mother's Clinic, Elaine speaking."

Stuart knew she was receiving an emergency call when she jackknifed into a sitting position and pushed her hair back from her face.

"Stuck? Calm down, Johnny. Everything is going to be okay. Where is she now?"

Listening carefully, Elaine's eyes narrowed as she tried to decipher Johnny's rambling.

Annette and Johnny had been down at the dock fishing. They'd run out of worms. Annette had volunteered to get them. Johnny was becoming increasingly incoherent. The worms were kept in a tub in the space beneath the floor joists of the house and the ground. He felt terrible because he'd teased her, calling her Winnie the Pooh and warning her not to take a honey pot with her or she'd probably get stuck. Moments after Annette had darted up the steps to the side of the house, he'd caught a whopper of a catfish. The next thing he knew, Annette was yelling that she was stuck in the opening and couldn't get out.

From the background, Elaine heard Annette say, "You laughed until you saw the blood."

"Blood?" Elaine asked. "Annette's bleeding?"

Between Johnny's self-recriminations for not getting the worms himself, Elaine gathered from his babbling that Annette had tried to back out from under the house and hit her head on one of the beams. Johnny had carried Annette into the house and wrapped her in several blankets.

"What's happened to Annette?" Stuart whispered, his system going on full alert.

Elaine motioned for Stuart to be quiet, then put her finger over her other ear. Two hysterical men talking to each other on the phone wouldn't help Annette one bit.

Fear for his sister's well-being knotted Stuart's stomach. Annette had always depended on him; he'd always been there when she'd needed him. Old habits die hard. He reached for the receiver, but Elaine batted his hand away.

"How's she feeling?"

Johnny wasn't sure. Annette hadn't taken the wound seriously. When he'd threatened to call a doctor, she'd insisted on his calling Elaine.

His voice lowered to a fearful whisper. "This won't cause a miscarriage, will it?"

"Nature has provided a safe cocoon for the baby," Elaine told him. "Stop blaming yourself and go back to Annette. Don't let her sleep and don't give her anything to drink. I'll get dressed and be there shortly."

Elaine started to hang up, but Stuart grabbed the receiver.

"Johnny? What the hell is going on out there?"

Between Stuart's "she what?" and "you what?" Elaine shot off the bed and scrambled into a pair of jeans and a sweatshirt. She gestured for Stuart to calm down. This wasn't the time for Stuart to fly off the handle. Johnny was scared and upset. She'd reassured Johnny, now Stuart was unnerving him.

"Did you call the hospital?" Stuart shouted. "You didn't! Dammit, Johnny—"

"Stuart!" Elaine protested. "For heaven's sake, will you let me get out there and see her before you go off half-cocked!"

"Never mind. I'll take care of it." Stuart banged the phone down, then picked it up, dialed for the operator and succinctly demanded the emergency number of the closest hospital.

Elaine grabbed for the phone to get his attention. From what she'd gathered from Johnny, Annette was in better shape than her husband. Neither Annette nor the baby was in immediate danger. "Dammit! She's my patient. I'll take care of her!"

"Yes, she's your patient." Stuart replied curtly. "But she's my sister. Johnny is practically incoherent. I couldn't make heads or tails out of anything he said. I'm sending for an ambulance."

"Men! The slightest thing happens to a pregnant woman and you think she's fatally wounded! Hang up the phone, Stuart. Your sister is my patient. I can handle this." Her eyes pleaded with him to reconsider. He responded by dialing the hospital's number. "Dammit, stop interfering!"

Shaking his head, Stuart began to give instructions on how to get to Annette's house. He realized he was riding roughshod over Elaine's feelings, but taking care of Annette was his first concern. It was a habit he couldn't change. Later, when he knew for certain Annette wasn't miscarrying, he'd reason with Elaine.

Elaine shot Stuart one last dirty look, then grabbed her medical bag and rushed through the door. She heard Stuart tell the person to whom he spoke that he'd drive directly to the hospital. She could have waited for him to get off the phone to try to reason with him, but she didn't. He'd arbitrarily excluded her from deciding what should be done for her patient. By damn, she wasn't going to stick around waiting for him!

Inside her car, she silently blasted Stuart for over-reacting as she raced toward Annette and Johnny's house. Stuart had attended several of her night classes; he knew how she felt about medical interference. Dammit, he'd had three months to personally witness how thorough and methodical she was with her patients. She never took chances with either the mother or the unborn child.

From the beginning he'd been reluctant to let his sister be attended by a midwife. By now, she thought, he should have learned to trust her judgment. Obviously he didn't.

Just who the hell did he think he was to step in and override her decision? The only things he knew about pregnancy and delivery were what she'd taught him. If he called an ambulance because Annette bumped her head, what would he do when Annette went into labor... call an ambulance and have her whisked into a hospital for delivery?

Elaine pressed harder on the gas pedal. She had to get to Annette's house before the ambulance arrived.

Minutes later she swerved onto the gravel lane leading to the lake house. Her heart sank when she saw blue lights circling at the end of the lane. The ambulance was already there.

She'd just slammed on the brakes when she saw Annette being carried on a stretcher toward the emergency vehicle. Johnny was holding her hand, whispering frantically.

Without wasting a moment, Elaine snatched her medical bag off the seat, opened her door and jogged to the back of the ambulance.

Using every ounce of her assertiveness, she physically blocked the back door of the ambulance and said, "I'm the patient's midwife. Take her back into the house, please."

Johnny dropped Annette's hand and rushed to her side. The blue lights overhead flashed across his distraught face. Unshed tears glistened in his eyes. Barely, just by a slender thread of control, he nodded his consent and gestured for the attendants to take his wife back inside.

"Do you want to be with her?" Annette inquired, following the man carrying the foot of the stretcher.

Again Johnny nodded. "Where's Stuart?"

"On his way to the hospital," she answered, grimacing as she caught a glance of Annette's face.

For a fraction of a second, Elaine experienced self-doubt. Blood oozed from the small cut at Annette's scalp line. A lump was starting to form. The black-and-blue bruise and the swelling were indicative of how hard she'd hit her head.

Prior experience and training came to Elaine's aid when she opened her medical bag. Facial contusions don't affect the baby, she reminded herself. She'd seen women who'd been in serious car accidents who hadn't suffered complications. She knew what to do, what signs to look for. Annette was in capable hands, despite what her brother thought.

The two men carrying Annette took her into her bedroom. After giving Elaine a skeptical glance, they skirted around Johnny and left the room, closing the door behind them.

Immediately Elaine set to work. While asking pertinent questions in a calm voice, she efficiently checked Annette's vital signs, then examined her. Annette wasn't in any danger. Her husband's hysterics had upset Annette more than the bump on her head.

One thing bothered Elaine: the size of the lump on Annette's head. From what she could gather, Annette must have been too stubborn to ask for help. Frustrated, forgetting the wooden beams immediately overhead, she'd straightened her back. Too late, she'd turned her head to the side and looked up. Elaine examined Annette's pupils for signs of concussion.

"The baby is doing fine," Elaine assured both parents as she began applying antiseptic to Annette's cut skin. "Hold still. This isn't going to sting."

"Should I tell the ambulance driver that we don't need them?" Johnny asked, his relief noticeable in his voice.

Elaine took another look at the swelling. "I don't like the looks of this lump. It's probably nothing to be alarmed over, but there is a slight chance of a mild concussion. Just to be on the safe side, I'd like to have her under overnight supervision at the hospital. Since the ambulance is here, I think you'll be more comfortable riding in it than going in the car. What do you think, Annette?"

"You're sure the baby is okay?" Johnny asked.

"Positive." Elaine touched Annette's hand to give her physical reassurance. She watched Annette glance toward her husband to see his reaction. "Taking you to the hospital is strictly a precautionary measure."

Johnny crossed the room, raised her hand to his lips and whispered, "Elaine probably wants to admit me for psychiatric observation. I must have sounded pretty crazy on the telephone."

Annette gave her husband a lopsided grin. "It's a good thing I'm having this baby at home. Johnny would probably get so shook up that he'd drive off to the hospital and leave me at the house."

"Never," Johnny responded immediately, dropping down on one knee and giving his wife a brief kiss. "I might get lost driving between here and Roanoke Rapids, but you'd be with me in the car."

Elaine gave Johnny an affectionate pat on his shoulders. "Under the circumstances, you did the right thing. You brought Annette inside and wrapped her in blankets to prevent her from going into shock, and then you called me. That's precisely what you should have done."

"You were wonderful," Annette agreed. She framed her husband's face with both of her hands. "Stop blaming yourself. It wasn't your fault that I got stuck. You did offer to get the worms."

"I should have insisted."

Elaine crossed to the door as she listened to the affectionate squabbling between Annette and her husband. Her hand was on the doorknob when she heard Annette giggle wickedly and ask, "What was Stuart doing at the clinic? Why didn't he drive you out here?''

Elaine chose to answer Annette's second question. "He'll be at the hospital."

Stuart paced under the canopy of the emergency entrance at the hospital. As he strode from one end of the admitting area to the other, he took turns silently cursing Johnny, Elaine and himself. What the hell had Johnny been thinking of when he'd allowed his pregnant wife down on the dock in the middle of the night? How many times had he warned Johnny about letting Annette flit up and down those steps? A dozen? A hundred? Each time he'd warned them he'd been pooh-poohed. Johnny should have known better than to let his pregnant wife climb under the house to get worms!

"I need the exercise," he muttered, mimicking his sister's voice. "Stop treating me like I'm an invalid. I'm just pregnant, not crippled. And I'm married, so stop bossing me around."

So help me, he silently roared, if anything happens to Annette or the baby because of Johnny's negligence I'll make him wish he'd never met my sister, much less married her.

Overwrought, he glanced toward the highway, expecting to see the ambulance's lights and hear a siren at any moment. Where are they? he wondered, fearing the worst.

The thought of his sister being in pain activated his vivid imagination. Would Elaine prevent the medical attendants from helping Annette? His sister was a baby when it came to pain. Breathing exercises wouldn't help if she was scared. He raked his hand through his hair, as though by doing so he could make the frightening picture he'd conjured up disappear.

Striding back toward the hospital's doors, he directed his animosity at Elaine. Granted, Annette was her patient, but dammit, this was an emergency. Why had she rushed off when she'd known an ambulance was on its way? Why couldn't she have waited until he'd dressed, then gone with him to the hospital? Stubborn pride, he answered with righteous indignation. Right now she was probably blocking the lane with her car while she told Annette to breath in and out.

He could still hear her accusation ringing in his ears. Interfering! "You're damned right I interfered," he grumbled. "What did she expect me to do? Go back to bed and knock off a few *z*'s? Ha!"

Just because Stuart loved Elaine didn't mean he loved his sister any less. And just because Annette was married didn't mean she wasn't his sister, his responsibility. His only sister. By God, she needed medical care. He'd gone against his better instincts once, but from here on out he'd make sure Annette got the proper attention...whether Johnny and Elaine thought it necessary or not!

Stuart shoved his hands deep into his pockets. The coins rattling in his pocket reminded him of one of the reasons Johnny and Annette had decided on a midwife: no hospitalization coverage. Johnny contacting a midwife was another example of his harebrained back-to-nature life-style. He should have put his foot down when they'd first mentioned the idea of having the baby at home, Stuart thought. He'd have gladly picked up the cost.

This was his fault. There was no one to blame but himself.

If he hadn't fallen head over heels for Elaine, he would have eventually convinced Annette that she and her baby deserved the best doctor in the area. Right now he'd feel one hell of a lot better if he knew Annette's regular doctor was inside, waiting for his sister to arrive.

He'd turned to pace toward the parking lot when he saw an ambulance, closely followed by Elaine's car, turning into the entrance. Why weren't the emergency lights and the siren on? Oh, God, they hadn't gotten there too late, had they? Had Annette gone into a coma and died? His heart was in his throat as he ran toward the ambulance, then backtracked as both vehicles passed by him.

Johnny climbed from the back of the ambulance, ahead of the attendants. He blocked Stuart from climbing inside the ambulance to personally check on his sister. "She's going to be okay. Elaine examined her at the house."

"The baby?"

"Fine," Johnny answered. He put his arm compassionately around Stuart's shoulder and guided him out of the way. "Maybe a concussion. Elaine wants her kept under medical supervision for the night. She contacted Dr. Kincaid before we left the house."

Elaine stepped from her car. Dr. Kincaid was striding to the stretcher as it was wheeled from the ambulance. She joined him beside the stretcher. "Annette, this is Dr. Kincaid."

Dr. Kincaid greeted the pregnant woman, smiling jovially and walking beside the stretcher. "Hello, young lady. I hear you got stuck and tried to use your head as a battering ram."

Annette grinned and raised her hand to the bump on her head. "I've always been hardheaded. Looks like I found the Easter egg I lost last year. It's a beauty, isn't it?"

"Gorgeous. Black and blue aren't my favorite colors, but never fear, in a couple of days your Easter egg will change colors." Dr. Kincaid glanced at Elaine. "Preliminary examination satisfactory?"

"Yeah. I just didn't want to take any chances," Elaine replied, dropping back as Johnny took his rightful place.

Stuart touched Elaine's elbow to get her attention. "Is the baby going to be okay?" he asked in a choked voice.

"In my opinion..." *Which doesn't mean anything to you.* "...both mother and child are fine." She was still too hurt and angry because of what he'd recently done to be more than stiffly polite. Pointedly she added, "Doctor Kincaid will keep you posted," and continued walking without glancing over her shoulder.

Stuart's steps faltered. He hadn't heard that cold tone in Elaine's voice for months. Inwardly he shuddered as icy fingers hopscotched up his spine. He'd been so wrapped up in worrying about Annette that he hadn't taken Elaine's feelings into account.

Apparently she was miffed, to put it mildly. He watched as Elaine, Annette and Dr. Kincaid vanished into the emergency room. Johnny was at the admitting desk answering questions and filling out forms. Stuart couldn't remember a time when he'd felt so totally useless.

Annette and Johnny had always depended on him. During the past few weeks, he'd thought he'd become somewhat indispensable to Elaine, also. All the people he cared most about in the world had walked away from him without a backward glance. Annette hadn't even spoken to him.

Stuart knew he had some explaining to do, but he didn't know where to start. He'd acted with the best of intentions. They had to know that, didn't they? He only wanted the best care possible for his sister. Did that make him a bad guy? There had been an emergency. He'd stepped in and taken charge. Wasn't that what they expected of him? While his whole world had tipped upside down, he'd behaved predictably.

"What did they expect of me?" he muttered, slamming his fist into his open palm. He crossed to an empty sofa and sagged onto it. He felt as though he were shattering into a million pieces and no one was going to bother sweeping him up.

During the next half hour, Stuart recalled exactly what had happened and where he'd heaped one mistake on top of another. He'd reacted rashly, he'd allowed himself to be guided only by his gut-level instincts. His sister had been in trouble, he'd had to help her. His intentions were pure; the results were what stank to high heaven.

He'd unintentionally insulted Elaine by striking at the solid foundation she'd built for herself in Tyler. For a stranger, moving into a small town, starting the Mother's Clinic solely on her own, building her self-esteem and gaining the love and respect of the towns-people hadn't been an easy task. He'd dealt her a double blow. "I love you" and "I don't trust you" weren't compatible. He'd told her he loved her and trusted her, but when it had come down to a crisis situation, he'd panicked.

Stuart tunneled his hands through his hair. How he wished there were an instant-replay button for an entire day... or that he could step into a time warp and wake up with Elaine smiling at him.

What the hell was he going to do to get back in Elaine's good graces? Apologize? He winced at the thought. One thing he'd learned about Elaine was that she seldom lost her temper, but when she did she had a hell of a time finding it again.

Deep in thought, Stuart didn't notice Johnny sitting down beside him.

"I just talked to Elaine. Annette is getting settled into a room," Johnny said, leaning back against the sofa's cushion. "Dr. Kincaid gave Annette the thumbs-up sign. God, what a relief. I can't tell you what went through my mind when I saw blood on your sister's face."

He cleared his throat huskily and turned toward Stuart. "I know you don't think I'm much of a husband for your sister, but I love her. I'd shrivel up and die if anything happened to her."

Studying Johnny's face, Stuart realized his brother-in-law wasn't being overly dramatic. Why hadn't he seen how much Johnny loved his sister? Because you were too busy knocking his unorthodox manner of living, he thought, answering his own query. You couldn't understand why Annette would marry anyone so different from her big brother.

"I owe you an apology, Johnny." He gauged the utter disbelief he saw registered on Johnny's face against his own feelings of desperately wanting to right old wrongs. Johnny's eyes were alert but wary. "I've been heavy-handed with my big-brother routine."

"You love her, too. I've never resented listening to your advice," Johnny replied sincerely.

"Loving someone doesn't give you the privilege of constantly interfering in their lives or their work."

Johnny shrugged. "You see something you think is wrong and you want to fix it. I wouldn't call that interfering...not exactly."

"What would you call it?"

Chuckling, Johnny rubbed the stubble on his jaw. "When you side with me I call it brotherly concern. When you side with Annette against me I call it putting your nose in where it doesn't belong."

"What would you call what I did tonight?"

"Frankly?"

"Yeah."

"Terrific. I was relieved," Johnny admitted. "I started to call an ambulance, but Annette started getting agitated. She said to call Elaine first. You know, sometimes I think women are stronger about certain things than men give them credit for. There she was, lying on the sofa, breathing in and out, not a tear on her face." He drew a deep, ragged breath and slowly exhaled. "And there I was, so scared I'd have called the devil and given him everything in the workroom if I'd thought he'd have answered." He clamped his hand on Stuart's forearm. "I'll give you credit for one thing. You raised one special lady. She's got heart."

"Just to keep the record straight," Stuart said, "you weren't the only person scared. I may have sounded like I knew what the hell I was doing, but I made one of the biggest mistakes of my life tonight."

Johnny noticed the lines etched around Stuart's mouth. The man had something eating at him. Annette would have considered this a red-letter day and marked it on the calendar if she'd heard Stuart apologize to him and confide in him, too.

"Wanna tell me about it?"

Stuart bent forward, resting his elbows on his knees and his head in his hands. He couldn't remember ever confiding in anyone about his personal affairs. Until Elaine had entered his life, he'd been self-sufficient, self-supporting and self-reliant. Now he wondered if perhaps there wasn't a dash of self-centeredness thrown in as a by-product of those positive traits. Wasn't it being self-centered to think he could solve everyone's problems and seldom share his own inner thoughts? He needed to talk to someone. Who could be better than a member of his own family?

Determined to show Johnny he trusted him, Stuart raised his head and answered, "Yeah. I do. Elaine and I have been living together."

Stuart paused, waiting for a reaction.

"Since the Fourth of July picnic," Johnny commented.

"I'm in love with her. To put it in your own words, she's got heart. I stepped on it tonight when I called an ambulance for Annette. Elaine told me I was interfering, but I didn't hear her until it was too late."

Johnny whistled between his teeth at Stuart's dilemma, then uttered an explicit curse.

Stuart sighed. "When you all arrived, she barely spoke to me. What the hell am I going to say or do to make things right between us?"

Elaine saw the two men with their heads close together. Johnny was talking; Stuart was listening intently. Usually it was the other way around: Stuart lectured, Johnny listened. At least something good came out of this, she thought, though she wasn't in a particularly forgiving mood.

Neither man noticed her as she turned and walked toward the side exit. She had a lot of thinking to do, and she wanted to do it alone. She'd done her job. Annette was resting comfortably. Dr. Kincaid said he'd notify the two men as to when they could go to her room.

Head bowed, she walked to her car. The splendid evening she'd planned had backfired. She'd intended to tell him she loved him, that she'd marry him, before she told him about their baby. Falling asleep and Johnny's phone call had destroyed those plans. When Stuart had placed the call to the hospital, Elaine had come close to hating him. He'd betrayed her, led her to believe he'd changed his mind about midwives and natural childbirth while silently doubting her competence.

Annette's emergency had been a test. He'd failed her miserably.

"Damn him," she whispered aloud. "We spend hours talking. It wasn't as though he didn't have a chance to tell me how he felt. He could have told me he had qualms when it came to his sister. Not once did he bring up the subject."

As she opened her car door, she wondered what he'd think about his child being born above the Mother's Clinic. Poetic justice? she mused, taking a liking to the extremely subtle form of revenge.

She started the car and headed toward Tyler. Wasn't it better that she knew now? If Annette hadn't gotten stuck, Elaine would have remained ignorant of his intentions. They'd have been married by the time Annette went into labor. He'd have whisked Annette off to the hospital, and Elaine would really have been in a mess.

"You're in a mess now," she murmured, glancing in the rearview mirror to see if anyone was following her.

A harsh laugh broke the silence in the car. Did she really expect Stuart to come charging after her? He'd chased her once. She seriously doubted that he considered her worthy of a second effort, not when their differences were irreconcilable.

Elaine sniffed, then wiped a tear from her eyelashes with the back of her hand. Tears? Self-pity? Was she feeling sorry for herself? She couldn't lie to herself.

"Yeah, you're a blubbering fool. Crying won't help. You've already learned that lesson, kiddo."

To distract herself from her thoughts, she reached to the dashboard and flicked on the stereo. The Bob York tape in the tape deck began playing a mournful melody, "Lost Lover." She punched the eject button. She didn't need the mellow tones of his saxophone to give her the blues. She already had a bad case . . . and she didn't know what to do to cure them.

An old remedy immediately popped into her mind: work.

Elaine was afraid work wouldn't cure her inner turmoil. Being around other pregnant women and their husbands while she was pregnant, without a husband, wouldn't be a remedy. Torture, she mused, sadly shaking her head.

There had to be a solution, but she couldn't think of one.

Chapter Ten

Elaine felt sharp claws kneading her chest. She opened one eye and gave Clunker a baleful glare as she moved the amorous cat aside. "Don't look at me as though I'm guilty of kitty abuse. In case you haven't noticed, I don't have hair on my chest. That hurts."

Vexed, Clunker blinked once, then tilted her nose toward the ceiling and swaggered to the pillow beside Elaine. She continued her morning ritual, which began with her sharpening her claws on Stuart's chest and ended with her washing herself with her raspy pink tongue. Usually she deigned to give Stuart a few licks in appreciation of his being her personal scratching post.

Elaine rubbed the sleep from her eyes and glanced at her wristwatch. She groaned aloud. Claire would arrive at the clinic in ten minutes. The thought of seeing her sunshiny smile was enough to elicit another groan from Elaine.

She spent her normal sleeping hours staring at the ceiling, wide-awake, futilely searching for a solution to her problems. Now, with her internal clock switched from a.m. to p.m., she wanted to pull the covers over her head and catch another forty winks.

Knowing Claire would be up the steps in two seconds flat, demanding to know if she was ill, gave Elaine the energy necessary to slowly swing her legs over the edge of the mattress. Half-asleep, she rolled to her feet and staggered to the bathroom.

"I feel good. I feel healthy. I look great." Her morning positive-thinking litany had a false ring.

One look in the mirror made Elaine wonder why she was trying to convince herself of the big lie. She felt awful and looked worse. She splashed cold water on her face and hoped it would have a reviving effect.

As she dried her face on a towel, she mentally scheduled her day. Aside from her normal work load, she needed to call the hospital to get a report on Annette. Fairly certain Annette would be home by noon, she decided she should be there when she arrived. Claire could cover for her at the clinic.

Raising her head, she stared at her reflection and asked, "What about Stuart?"

"Yeah, what about Stuart?" she heard repeated from the bedroom.

Startled, she spun around and poked her head out of the bathroom. Her eyes rounded in surprise when she saw him sprawled on her bed with Clunker curled up on his chest.

"How...?" she sputtered, tossing the wet towel into the sink and moving to the side of the bed.

Stuart reached into his pocket and tossed the key to the front door of the clinic on her bed. "I considered coming through the window, but I decided the conventional manner of entering a building might keep the police department from shooting at me."

"Pardon me if I don't laugh at your jokes. I seem to have misplaced my sense of humor this morning." Deftly grabbing the key off the bed, she started to shove it into her pocket. There were no pockets in her nightgown. She considered dropping it down the front of her nightie then decided against it. She tossed the key on the dresser.

"A key makes entering simpler, but it isn't necessary." Stuart scratched Clunker behind the ears. She snuggled under his chin and began purring. "The hard part was working up my nerve to make an appearance."

"You don't look the least bit nervous," Elaine commented. Striding to the closet, she took out her robe and slipped into it.

"Looks can be deceiving."

"Actions aren't," she countered.

"Why don't you sit down, and we'll discuss my reactions." Stuart patted the bed where she'd previously lain. When she sat down primly on the edge of the chair, his courage slipped a notch. He'd spent the night parked outside, fretting. He'd made peace with Johnny and Annette. From the look on Elaine's face, the only peace he was going to get from her would be a piece of her mind.

Elaine stared at Stuart, really looking at him. She avoided his dark, compelling eyes and the sensuous curve of his lips. She concentrated on his clothing. He was wearing the same slacks and shirt he'd worn to the hospital. For a man who seldom had a hair out of place or a wrinkle in his clothing, he was amazingly disheveled. She wondered if he'd spent the night at the hospital. Nobody could have stopped him from sleeping on a couch in the waiting room if he'd thought Annette might have a relapse.

Brotherly love, she mused. Last night he'd had to choose between what he'd judged as the best for his sister's welfare and trusting Elaine. Years of loving combined with years of training had weighed heavily against her. Although she'd lost, she couldn't fault him for loving his sister.

He thinks you're a quack, she reminded herself when she felt a peculiar sensation in the region of her heart. Annette was your patient. He should have trusted you.

"I don't blame you for loving your sister... for wanting to take care of her. I do blame you for interfering with my work."

"Guilty on both counts," he agreed, refusing to defend himself. He deserved her recriminations. At her worst, she couldn't say anything he hadn't already told himself.

"Didn't you think I was capable of examining Annette and determining whether or not she needed to be hospitalized?"

"I didn't think; I reacted. Rote performance. Conditioning. When Annette was twelve, she fell out of a tree and broke her arm. I called an ambulance. When she was fifteen, she thought the sliding door was open and struck her hand through the plate glass. I called an ambulance. When she wrecked her car and couldn't move her neck . . . I called an ambulance. Last night, when Johnny called, I wasn't thinking. I did what I've always done."

"Called an ambulance," Elaine concluded for him. "But Annette isn't a child. She isn't your responsibility. The circumstances were different."

"This time I was totally . . . predictably . . . wrong." He gently moved Clunker off his chest and sat up.

"You'd do the same thing again, wouldn't you?" Elaine watched as her barbed question hit its mark. He'd wronged her. He'd admitted it. Why was she feeling as though she were the one fighting unfairly? Why wasn't he fighting back, defending what he'd done?

Stuart paused. He could promise never to interfere, but he'd be guilty of making false promises. The thought of someone dear to his heart being in pain, suffering, made his blood run cold.

"Yes, I probably would grab the phone and call an ambulance."

Stuart crossed from the bed to the front window. Rubbing the back of his neck, he struggled to openly share with Elaine the reason for his actions.

He wondered why it was so much easier to cope with Elaine's fears than with his own? He hadn't been appalled when she'd told him she couldn't have children. Nor had he thought less of her because she'd secretly feared that her marriage had left an invisible scar: frigidity. Why couldn't he tell her why he'd insisted on calling an ambulance? Until last night, when he'd talked to Annette, he hadn't realized the reason behind his own fears.

Glancing at Elaine, he knew she'd heard him, but he also knew he'd given her an unsatisfactory reply. She understood, but she couldn't accept the knowledge that he'd probably react in exactly the same manner. Regardless of whether she thought less of him or not, he had to tell her the whole truth.

"Did Annette tell you what happened to our parents?" he asked.

"No." Thinking she had heard all he had to say, she was mentally preparing herself to ask him to leave. Trust and faith were the foundation of love, just as a strong medical background was the foundation of her career. By disclosing his conditioned response to any emergency, he'd cracked all her underpinnings. She seriously doubted that their relationship could be cemented back together, but she had to listen to anything else he had to say. Above all else, she wanted him to vindicate his actions. "She mentioned that you'd raised her. That's all."

"I think she purposely blocked it from her memory. God knows I did." He rammed his hands into his pockets. As if it were a nightmare that could only be remembered in snatches, he began recalling what had happened. "We'd gone to Florida during Christmas vacation. Outside of Atlanta we were caught in a freak ice- and snowstorm. Dad had been driving until we pulled off the highway to get gas."

He pulled his hand from his pocket and looked at it. "Funny, I remember all of us standing around the soda machine, comparing tans while the gas attendant filled the tank. Laughing." His head cocked to one side. "Yeah. I can remember how Mom laughed when Dad asked her if she still had a sunburn behind her knees."

He'd not only blocked out the tragic ending of the trip, he'd blocked the good times, too. Talking to Elaine brought bold images of his mother and father to mind.

"I could tell Dad was tired, so I offered to drive. He tossed me the keys and told Annette to get in the front seat. Dad teased Mom, saying he was going to inspect her for strap marks."

Stuart stopped, as though suddenly aware that he wasn't in the room alone. "You'd have liked my folks. I wonder if one of the reasons I haven't married is because I wouldn't settle for less than what they had. Mom used to say that marriage was more than finding a roommate. You had to find a soul mate. Someone who could see your weak spots but love you anyway."

Elaine couldn't reply. A woman wanted a man she could respect and admire, but personally she thought that living with someone who had no flaws or vulnerabilities would be a tremendous strain.

"Forgive me for digressing," he said, going back into his past. "Where was I?"

"About to get behind the wheel and drive," Elaine answered.

His lips tightened across his teeth. "Yeah. I was driving. It happened on the ramp leading to the highway. One minute we were curving, going downhill, and the next minute the tires hit an ice patch and we were airborne. On impact the doors flew open. I was thrown out one side, Annette flew out the other side. The snow broke our fall."

Stuart closed his eyes, remembering free-falling, feeling the air knocked out of his lungs, fighting to catch his breath. And then he'd heard it: his dad's shouts, the explosion, and Annette's piercing scream. Stuart's mouth twisted into an anguished grimace.

"Mom and Dad were trapped in the back seat and couldn't get out. I remember running through the thigh-deep snow, circling the car, trying to help them. It was Annette, a twelve-year-old kid, who ran down to the highway. A trucker stopped and radioed for help. I've always believed that had I gotten help soon enough, they might be alive today."

Compassion wrung her heart until tears blinded her. "Oh, Stuart, it wasn't your fault. It was an accident."

"Yeah." He sighed, feeling a weight lift from his shoulders when he heard Elaine speak. "But I blamed myself. I'd look at Annette and feel guilty for depriving her of a mother and father. I tried to make it up to her by being there any time she needed me. I guess somewhere along the line I became overly protective. I couldn't . . . can't . . . bear the thought of her being in pain and me not being able to do anything to help her."

Barefoot, Elaine soundlessly crossed the room and stood behind Stuart. She put her hands on his back, letting him feel her presence. His muscles were taut. Lightly she pressed her face against his shoulder.

"It was an accident," she repeated softly. "I understand why you feel guilty. I lived with horrible guilt feelings when the doctor diagnosed my tubal pregnancy. I felt as though I'd cheated my husband by being unable to give him a child. When I couldn't get pregnant, I blamed myself again. Don't you see, Stuart? Neither of us could stop what happened, but we both blamed ourselves. It happened. It's over. Let it go.''

Stuart shifted, drawing her against his chest. ''Annette said the same thing. Oh, Elaine, I don't want to lose you, but I can't promise not to panic when she goes into labor. I know what can happen if she has complications and isn't in a hospital. I could lose her.''

''You've got to trust my judgment. I've delivered hundreds of babies. I know when a woman is at risk.''

Hugging Elaine, he nodded reluctantly. ''That didn't keep me from being scared witless last night. At least I won't have to worry about you going through labor and delivery. Unlike your former husband, I'm almost glad you can't have children.''

Elaine felt her heart constrict. He didn't want their baby? No, she screamed silently, grasping his shoulders when her knees buckled. For the first time in her life, she fainted.

From a great distance, Elaine could hear Stuart shouting. Claire, yes, he was calling Claire. She tried to raise her arm, to speak, to let him know she wasn't seriously ill, but she couldn't. The warm blackness that had unexpectedly sucked her into its vortex edged closer, swirled, then created an impenetrable fog.

''I think I'd better call an ambulance,'' Stuart abruptly informed Claire, simultaneously reaching for the phone. ''One minute we were talking and . . . she just collapsed.''

Claire touched Elaine's forehead. "Skip calling the ambulance. Find her black satchel and bring it to me."

Immobilized by fear, Stuart's eyes scanned the room until he located the medical bag. He heard Claire speak, but his body wouldn't function properly. The phone dropping back in its cradle drew Claire's attention to him.

"Stuart! Move!" Claire held Elaine's wrist and took her pulse rate. Gently she raised her eyelid. "She doesn't seem to have a fever. Her pulse is a little fast, but still within the normal range. She's fainted."

"Fainted?" Stuart felt damned woozy himself. "Is she anemic or something?"

"Not to my knowledge. She looks exhausted."

"My sister got herself into a jam last night and wound up banging her head. Elaine was up half the night taking care of her."

"Is Annette okay? And the baby?"

"They're fine. What about Elaine?" He knelt beside the bed and picked up her limp hand.

"You keep an eye on her. I'll get something to bring her around."

Elaine felt as though she were floating, rising to the surface. Disoriented, she held tightly to the hand in hers as she gradually opened her eyelids. She knew something important had happened, but she couldn't remember exactly what.

"Elaine, sweetheart . . ."

Her dark eyelashes fluttered as she wondered why Stuart was pale and unshaven. He looked physically ill. She tried to talk, but her mouth was too dry. She licked her lips.

"Water? I'll get you some." Stuart shot to his feet and around the end of the bed.

The fog that had blanketed her mind slowly lifted, revealing what she'd been unable to accept. Stuart didn't want children. Elaine buried her fist against her mouth to keep from screaming. Her other hand defensively covered her lower abdomen.

She'd been too greedy. She'd asked for Stuart's love, and then she'd wished for a child. Oh, God, she silently wailed, couldn't she have both?

Claire took the half-empty glass of water from Stuart's hand as she entered the room. "Go downstairs. There's coffee in the urn. I'll take care of Elaine."

"No." He wasn't going to leave Elaine's bedside until she was back on her feet.

"I want to examine her, and I need privacy," Claire stated firmly. "You look like you're going to flip out, too. I don't need two patients."

Stuart wiped his wet hand on his shirttail. Silently cursing himself for being inept when someone he loved needed him, he strode through the door.

Putting her arm under Elaine's shoulder for support, Claire raised her head and put the glass to her lips. "You're pregnant."

Elaine nodded, then took a sip. "How did you find out?"

"While I was in the office bathroom I saw the empty box in the trash can. A pregnancy test kit. Simple mathematics." She lowered Elaine's head back onto the pillows. "One and one make three, huh?"

"I wanted to tell you, but I thought Stuart should be the first to know."

"I'm surprised he's not the one flat on his back in a dead faint," Claire responded dryly. "You did tell him, didn't you?"

"No."

"No? Why not? He's the baby's father, for heaven's sake!"

"Shhhh!" Elaine covered her friend's mouth with one finger.

"Don't shush me," Claire whispered furiously after she'd moved Elaine's finger aside. "Why haven't you told him?"

"I couldn't. Annette got hurt and he called an ambulance." From Claire's puzzled expression, Elaine knew she must not have made sense. "He interfered between me and a patient!"

"So? Annette's his sister. You've known all along that he wasn't a proponent of natural childbirth."

"Don't you understand? He had good reasons for falling apart when he thinks his sister is in danger, but . . . I'm a midwife! He'll rush me to the hospital to deliver our baby! How many patients will trust me, knowing that?"

"Oh." Claire reached into the pocket of her blouse for a piece of gum. She needed something she could sink her teeth into.

"Please. No gum. One snap—crackle—pop and I'll have the screaming meemies."

"Sorry. It helps me think." Claire put the packet of gum back in her pocket and began chewing her thumbnail. "I could tell him."

"I'm the one who's pregnant. I have to tell him, not you. But telling him only solves half the problem." Wearily she closed her eyes. She couldn't tell him this morning. He'd think she despised him for revealing his vulnerability, which wasn't the case. "He'll feel honor-bound to marry me immediately."

"Don't confuse the issue by bringing up his honor. It's as plain as the nose on your face that he loves you. Of course he'll want to marry you." Claire snapped her fingers as inspiration struck. "So, don't tell him you're pregnant until after you're married. Let him think you're just gaining weight."

"Come on, Claire. He isn't blind or stupid. Being pregnant isn't something I can hide."

"That's it! Hide. Leave town until you have the baby and then come back. I saw that happen on one of the nighttime soaps. The heroine came back, the hero divorced the woman he'd married . . . uh-oh, bad idea, huh?"

"Terrible." Elaine groaned and rolled her eyes toward the ceiling. "I need fewer complications, not additional ones. I have to tell him. I can't build a marriage on a foundation of deceit."

Claire pulled the sheet up to Elaine's chin and rose from the bed. "You don't have to tell him today. You're staying right here in bed. Don't shake your head. Of all people, a midwife knows a woman needs to rest in the first trimester of pregnancy. You don't have anything scheduled that I can't handle."

"You can't handle Stuart. He won't be satisfied until he sees that I haven't barred the door while he wasn't looking."

"You stop worrying about everyone else and take care of yourself for a change."

Claire left the room, closing the door. She wasn't going to let anyone cross that threshold, including Dr. Cimarron.

Late the same afternoon, Elaine awoke feeling like a new woman. Sleep had provided her with the rest she'd needed and her subconscious had provided her with a solution: *love.*

"I love him," she murmured, tossing back the sheet and crossing to the closet. Deciding she'd wear something tailored, she selected a cream-colored two-piece suit and a emerald-green silk blouse. "And he loves me."

She realized they both had flaws. She procrastinated; he was impulsive. She preferred to run and hide when she was hurt; Stuart preferred an immediate confrontation. She worried; he jumped to conclusions.

She also realized they both had strengths—shared strengths. Professionally, they both were dedicated. They both cared about the welfare of others. They both had guilt feelings they'd carried alone, unable to let the people they loved share the burden.

They were different, and yet they were alike.

"What I must do is accentuate the positive and eliminate the negative." Elaine grinned as she put the finishing touches on her makeup. "Another Bob York oldie-but-goodie."

She wasn't going to build insurmountable barriers to keep from being hurt. She was going to take the advice she gave her patients: relax and let nature take its course.

Spirits high, she opened the bedroom window so Clunker could come and go as she wished. She rashly considered taking the fire escape to avoid Claire but decided against it.

Claire couldn't stop her. No one could.

Or so she thought until she saw Claire bodily blocking the bottom of the steps.

"And just where do you think you're going?" she asked, stretching her arms out to the banister and the wall. She blew a bubble and let it pop. She didn't lower her arms.

"I have a dentist appointment."

"Uh-uh. Your dentist is on vacation. You're not running out of here without me knowing where you're going. Stuart said he'd have my head on a silver platter if I let you out of my sight."

"I'm not running away from Stuart this time. I'm running to him. He's the dentist I'm going to see."

Claire swallowed her gum. "Did I swallow my gum down the wrong pipe, or is it the sound of wedding bells I hear ringing in my ears?"

"Wedding bells." Elaine grabbed Claire and gave her a hearty hug. "Close the clinic and get yourself a bridesmaid's dress. There's going to be a wedding soon, and we're both going to be in it."

"You're the boss lady. You run along. I wouldn't want you to miss your appointment."

Thirty minutes of uninterrupted Bob York music later, Elaine marched into Stuart's office. She hadn't allowed herself to think about what she'd say or how Stuart would react. She didn't care if the whole world knew she was chasing him.

"Elaine, I wasn't expecting you," June said as Elaine came through the office door. "Are you here for business or pleasure?"

"Both. It's an emergency appointment. Can you squeeze me in?"

June glanced at the clock behind her desk. "He had one more appointment scheduled in a few minutes, but it's a man who usually cancels at the last minute. Do you want me to tell Stuart that you're here?"

"No. I'd rather surprise him."

Elaine could feel her heart pounding in her chest as she strode down the narrow hallway leading to the examination room. She raised her hand to knock on the partially closed door. Please, please help me say the right things, she prayed silently.

She uncurled the fist she'd made and pushed the door open.

Stuart glanced up, expecting June to usher in his next patient. He was on his feet in a flash. "Elaine, what are you doing here?"

"I've come to see you about braces," she improvised, smiling.

"For that one crooked little tooth? I really don't think—"

"I insist."

Stuart shrugged. He didn't have the faintest idea why she'd arrived unannounced, but from the brightness shining in her eyes he knew braces weren't the reason for her unprecedented visit. Before he could close the gap between them, Elaine was stretched out on the dental chair with her mouth open.

"You're making me nervous," he confided as he closed the door.

"Don't you have that backward? I'm the one who's supposed to be nervous. I'm the patient."

"The doctor's hands are shaking." He held both hands toward her. "This morning you fainted in my arms, and this afternoon you're bright eyed and bushy tailed? And you came to me? I have this gut feeling that you aren't here professionally."

"In a way, I am." Professionally she was a midwife. She was here to tell him about their baby. She hadn't lied. She'd just walked around the truth a little bit.

She took his hands and tugged until Stuart bent over her. Then she released them and framed his face. "I love you, Dr. Cimarron."

"I love you, too," he whispered, closing his lips over hers.

Very thoroughly he examined her mouth. His tongue gently probed each crevice, then traced over the edges of her teeth. Her teeth were perfect, even the crooked one.

When he raised his head fractionally, Elaine whispered, "No anesthetic, please. I'm going to have your baby."

Stuart gripped the arms of the chair to keep from falling forward. His mind went momentarily blank, then began spinning in crazy circles. "You're what? I thought . . . you said . . ."

"I'm pregnant. I didn't think I'd ever say those wonderful words, but it's true. I'm definitely p.g."

"I'd better sit down before I fall down." Stuart grabbed his stool and rolled it beside her. "You're sure? You've seen a—"

"Professional midwife. Any objections?"

Slowly the reason for her visit sank into his thick skull. She'd come to see him—one professional to another professional—dentist and midwife.

He couldn't answer her impulsively. Their future as man and wife was hanging by a slender thread. One wrong word and she wouldn't want him—or braces.

Elaine watched his brow wrinkle as he measured his words. She could wait. Patience was one of her strong points, haste was one of his flaws.

His hands splayed over her stomach. "A baby."

"Our baby. Yours and mine." She covered his hand with hers.

"I'm delighted . . . no, thrilled."

His smile dazzled her. "Me, too. I was going to tell you last night."

"Before Annette's accident?" He leaned closer, brushing his hand over her hair as she nodded. "I wish I'd known."

"I'm glad you didn't. I would never have understood why you're so protective of Annette if you hadn't explained this morning."

"Sweetheart, I love you dearly. But I don't think I can change. If you skinned your knee I'd probably call an ambulance quicker than you could get a Band-Aid."

Elaine shook her head. "Programmed behavior can be changed. You've taught yourself how to react in a crisis situation by using negative thinking. Mentally you're saying, 'I'm helpless. I'll get help.' You aren't helpless, and neither am I. We've survived when people who weren't strong would have given up."

What she'd said made sense to Stuart. If you think you can win, you will win. If you think you're going to lose, you become a loser.

"Do you want it in writing before you marry me?" he asked, grinning devilishly and rolling his chair backward to his work counter. He picked up a pad and pencil and hastily wrote a message.

"A prenuptial agreement?"

Stuart ripped the top sheet off the pad, then stood. He hauled Elaine out of the chair and into his arms. He stuck the note in front of her face. "Yeah, sweetheart, a prenuptial agreement that you can stash alongside my résumé and an album filled with baby pictures."

Quickly Elaine read the note aloud. "Positive Thinking List. Elaine marries Stuart. They have a healthy baby. They live happily ever after."

And they did.

* * * * *

ATTRACTIVE, SPACE SAVING BOOK RACK

Display your most prized novels on this handsome and sturdy book rack. The hand-rubbed walnut finish will blend into your library decor with quiet elegance, providing a practical organizer for your favorite hard-or soft-covered books.

Only $9.95

Approximately 16" x 8" when assembled

Assembles in seconds!

To order, rush your name, address and zip code, along with a check or money order for $10.70* ($9.95 plus 75¢ postage and handling) payable to *Silhouette Books*.

Silhouette Books
Book Rack Offer
901 Fuhrmann Blvd.
P.O. Box 1396
Buffalo, NY 14269-1396

Offer not available in Canada.

BKR-2A

*New York and Iowa residents add appropriate sales tax.

Silhouette Intimate Moments

Rx: One Dose of

DODD MEMORIAL HOSPITAL

In sickness and in health the employees of Dodd Memorial Hospital stick together, sharing triumphs and defeats, and sometimes their hearts as well. Revisit these special people this month in the newest book in Lucy Hamilton's Dodd Memorial Hospital Trilogy, *After Midnight*—IM #237, the time when romance begins.

Thea Stevens knew there was no room for a man in her life—she had a young daughter to care for and a demanding new job as the hospital's media coordinator. But then Luke Adams walked through the door, and everything changed. She had never met a man like him before—handsome enough to be the movie star he was, yet thoughtful, considerate and absolutely determined to get the one thing he wanted—Thea.

Finish the trilogy in July with *Heartbeats*—IM #245.

Silhouette Special Edition

**In May, Silhouette SPECIAL EDITION
shoots for the stars with six heavenly romances
by a stellar cast of Silhouette favorites....**

Nora Roberts
celebrates a golden anniversary—her 50th Silhouette
novel—and launches a delightful new family series, THE
O'HURLEYS! with *THE LAST HONEST WOMAN* (#451)

Linda Howard
weaves a delicious web of FBI deceit—and slightly embellished
"home truths"—in *WHITE LIES** (#452)

Tracy Sinclair
whisks us to Rome, where the jet set is rocked by a cat
burglar—and a woman is shocked by a thief of hearts—in
MORE PRECIOUS THAN JEWELS (#453)

Curtiss Ann Matlock
plumbs the very depths of love as an errant husband attempts
to mend his tattered marriage, in *WELLSPRING* (#454)

Jo Ann Algermissen
gives new meaning to "labor of love" and "Special Delivery"
in her modern medical marvel *BLUE EMERALDS* (#455)

Emilie Richards
sets pulses racing as a traditional Southern widow tries to run
from romance California-style, in *A CLASSIC ENCOUNTER*
(#456)

**Don't miss this dazzling constellation of romance stars in
May—Only in Silhouette SPECIAL EDITION!**

*previously advertised as *MIRRORS*